SIST

After working happily for 'Dr Mac' at
Greyrigg Manor, Sister Amy Taggart
wasn't sure how she would stand up to
the take-over by his son Chris. Dr Chris
MacFarlane had never been to Greyrigg,
didn't know any of the staff, and didn't
care about the residents or what *they*
wanted—but that didn't stop him talking
about sweeping changes and 'improvements'. Hadn't Amy better get out before
it all broke her heart?

Lancashire born, Jenny Ashe read English at Birmingham, returning thence with a BA and RA—the latter being rheumatoid arthritis, which after barrels of various pills, and three operations, led to her becoming almost bionic, with two manmade joints. Married to a junior surgeon in Scotland, who was born in Malaysia, she returned to Liverpool with three Scottish children when her husband went into general practice in 1966. She has written non-stop after that—articles, short stories and radio talks. Her novels just had to be set in a medical environment, which she considers compassionate, fascinating and completely rewarding.

Jenny Ashe has written seven other Doctor Nurse Romances, the most recent being *The Pagoda Doctors*, *The Partnership* and *Surgeon in the Clouds*.

SISTER AT GREYRIGG

BY
JENNY ASHE

MILLS & BOON LIMITED
ETON HOUSE   18–24 PARADISE ROAD
RICHMOND   SURREY TW9 1SR

CHAPTER ONE

AMY TAGGART vaulted over the drystone wall into the long meadow. The grey stones touched with green glowed in the early sun, as she crossed the field that led from the narrow Lakeland road to the shores of Daweswater with her usual bouncy steps. Not that she felt bouncy; a funeral wasn't the nicest thing to be happening on such a beautiful shining morning. But her natural good health and animal enjoyment of the clear air made her step light nonetheless. And using the stile took too long; vaulting was quicker. 'Come on, Nell!' The black and white collie leapt after her with equal zest, and they ran as they neared the village, where the general store was already open.

'Morning, Amy. You'll not be that grand today, Dr Mac being buried and all?' Mr Gately had the papers ready as usual. 'Anything else, love?'

Amy shook her head. 'It seems awfully empty at the Manor without him. Greyrigg won't ever be the same again.' She checked absently through the pile of newspapers, though Mr Gately never made a mistake—a *Times*, a *Guardian*, a *Telegraph* and three tabloids. There were eighteen residents at Greyrigg Manor at present, and their tastes were varied. She sighed. 'The Major won't have anyone to help him with the *Times* crossword now.'

'I hear his son's taking over?'

'His son inherits the Manor, but what he intends to do, we have no idea. He hasn't even bothered to come and see us—just got his secretary to phone and let us know he would be at the funeral.'

'We'll get a look at him, then?'

'Just briefly, I suppose,' said Amy. 'He's got a Harley Street practice, so he isn't likely to stick around for long.

Let's hope so anyway. We don't need outsiders.'

'What's his name, do you know?'

'Christopher James Fairlie MacFarlane.' Amy's pretty nose wrinkled at the mouthful. 'Oh dear, what a difference from dear old Dr Mac! And no one could have such a kindly heart. His patients were his children. No one could look after old folk like him.'

'There never was a better man,' agreed Mr Gately. 'I'll be shutting shop for funeral. His heart was in Daweswater, there's no denying.'

Amy picked up her bundle. 'See you at the church, then, Mr Gately.'

'Aye, you will and all—and the rest of village, happen.'

'Come on, Nell.' The bitch had been sniffing around the shop, her fringed tail waving heartily at the familiar smells of string and paper, of dog biscuits and coffee.

They walked more slowly back. Amy looked around her at the familiar fells, clear against the cloudless sky, purple with heather and green with bracken at its best. She had only been away from Daweswater when she was training in Lancaster. She had thought she was beginning to enjoy living in a town, but when the job of Warden of Greyrigg Manor had come up, she knew this was where she wanted to be. She breathed in deeply, feeling tears not far away at the thought of that pale oak coffin that held what was left on earth of dear Dr Mac. The skylarks were singing in full-throated joy. And the sheared sheep looked strangely thin beside their almost fully grown lambs still in their curly fleeces. They bleated to each other, the sound carrying across the still valley.

The water of the lake shone through the trees, reflecting the fells in every detail, the bright sunlight sides and the deep shadows. In spite of her grief—or perhaps because of it—Amy felt a deep sense of belonging to this beauty and peace.

She climbed the stile on the way back, though Nell cleared the wall as usual—one didn't vault with an armful of newspapers. They set off the few yards of road before the high stone gateposts of the elegant drive up to the Manor. There was a rattling, coughing sound of a very elderly lorry, Billy Braithwaite's milk lorry. Amy whistled to Nell, who slipped obediently behind her mistress. The lorry slowed down as Bill spotted Amy. The window was down, and he leaned an elbow on it and grinned. 'Nice day again, Amy.'

'Lovely. I was first to the village today, Billy. What kept you?'

He grinned again. They had a standing joke, about who was first at the village. 'I overslept—late night last night.'

'You'd better break a few records if you're going to make it to the funeral.'

Billy's agreeable sunburnt face turned solemn. 'I won't miss paying my respects.' He released the hand-brake, lifted a brown hand in farewell, and pressed the accelerator.

Amy knew the tiny whitewashed church would be full today. She turned to the drive, shaded by conifers and yew. The sign, 'Home for Retired Gentlefolk', had been there since she remembered the place. She wondered if the new owner, Dr MacFarlane junior, would want it renewed. She had never thought that necessary before. Old Dr Mac didn't give a damn, as he himself said; he was here to care about the happiness and well-being of his guests, as he always called them. He wasn't trained as a geriatrician, but his knowledge and skill had turned him into an acknowledged expert. Amy had learned from him all about compassion, about human love and tenderness to those weaker than the norm. She could never be grateful enough to him, the angel of Greyrigg with white hair and a briar pipe.

The Manor was a graceful grey stone building, covered in parts by Virginia creeper. Some of the windowframes were showing signs of neglect, and the gravel paths were well sprinkled with weeds. Arthur Taylor, the handyman and gardener, wasn't as young as he used to be. Yet he also had learned from Dr Mac, and could often be seen wheeling Ruby Barton in her chair to the place she loved under the chestnut trees across the untidy lawn, or even putting little Aggie Brown on the swing under the oak and giving her a few playful pushes, to her enormous delight. He would spend his gardening time fetching rugs and books and cups of tea. And bearing in mind Dr Mac's creed, Amy had never made any protest. Would the new Dr Mac change that too?'

The carved mahogany staircase gleamed mellow in the sun. Amy put the papers on the sideboard and ran upstairs, Nell making her own way thirstily to the kitchen for her biscuits and water. Amy never used the lift, feeling somehow that while she had her health and strength, she should be grateful for it by using her limbs. Her large room with its own small bathroom was on the second floor. The residents weren't getting up yet, but she could hear Olive Park and Daniel Feather, the two nurses on duty at eight, laughing as they took their own breakfast, before taking tea to the guests, and getting them up. The laughter echoed up the staircase, as Amy stood outside Dr Mac's room, the one next to hers. Perhaps there was no need to be sad; he must surely be there, in that sunny room. He had lived there so long, neglecting his real home away near Keswick. He was now part of the sunshine, part of the laughter, part of the friendly ghosts who whispered about the Manor on windy nights, and made the place feel warm and safe.

Then she heard a noise inside the room. Silly—who could be there now? She went to the door and pushed it wider, peeping inside. There, standing shakily with the aid of a stick, Aggie Brown gazed out of the window, her usually cheeky blue eyes full of tears. 'Aggie dear, you know you shouldn't have come up without help,' Amy scolded gently. 'You might have fallen.'

'I know, lass, I know.' She took a step away from the window, and Amy ran to take her arm and help her to the door. The tears spilled over on to her faded pink cheeks, and Amy hadn't the heart to scold her, though she was always disobeying the rules. 'I had to come and say goodbye to him—private like.'

'I understand, Aggie dear. But you mustn't miss breakfast, so off you go. And don't forget your Glurenorm. Olive might have been round with the tablets already.'

'I couldn't take any breakfast, lass.'

'Just a spot, Aggie. I can't take you to the funeral if you haven't eaten—you know how your low blood sugar makes you dizzy.'

Olive Park was looking for Aggie, and took her from Amy halfway downstairs. Amy went back to her room, where she took a quick shower. She came out in her cotton housecoat and went to the open window to breathe in deeply the scented air, laden with sweet bracken and spruce tree scents, and the smell of the warm grass. The skylark was singing as though he could never sing loud enough to express his joy, and the lazy bees droned and grumbled in the creeper under Amy's window.

If only the new owner of the Manor would leave things exactly as they were! But it was hardly likely. And if the young Dr Mac did make changes, would she still want to stay here, still want to be Warden of Greyrigg? She venerated what Dr Mac had built up, felt the satisfaction of living in a homely and friendly community, where what she did was valued, and what she said obeyed. She gazed out, not seeing the wandering ram with curling horns who had rambled in to see if the grass in the Manor garden were sweeter than on the fellside.

Mary Ledbetter brought in her tray. Amy always ate in her room when she wasn't needed downstairs. It was convenient for Gwyn, the cook, and it enabled her to deal with the mail in private, for her downstairs office was open to all who wanted to wander in. Mary set the tray down and stopped to chat, as she often did. Today there was only one topic of conversation. 'Have you a black dress, Amy?' she asked.

'No. But I've got a grey cotton suit that will look all

right with a dark blouse. And I'll wear that little black straw hat, I think. How can we show enough respect? Nothing can express it, can it, Mary?'

'No.' All the staff had been with them for years. Mary's face was wan. 'You think my black barathea would be all right? The one I bought when I did my jury service in 1983?'

'Great.' Amy spread some marmalade on her brown toast. 'I suppose Gwyn has started on the buffet?'

'Oh aye. She's made two lots of rolls, and some oatmeal biscuits. Pastries she's doing just before church, then they'll be still warm from the oven.' They both sat silent for a moment, thinking of Greyrigg Manor without Dr Mac. Mary sniffed. 'Liked his oatmeal biscuits . . .' And she suddenly got up to go, muttering something about 'getting on', and Amy heard her sniffing again on her way down. Dr Mac did like oatmeal biscuits, and like the gentleman he was, he always made a point of thanking Gwyn Jones when she made them. It would be a very long time before any of them stopped thinking about Dr Mac.

Amy drank her coffee, and counted mentally how many of the eighteen residents were coming in the mini-bus. Olive would make sure that those who were had extra care with their dressing. Amy took her tray down, and had a word with Gwyn before going to the dining room to help make sure everyone was smart. She sat with them, selfconscious in her little straw hat, and tried to sound confident that the new Dr Christopher MacFarlane wouldn't make any changes in their lives. 'He's a busy man, probably can't wait to get back to London.'

Faith Hindle arrived next, with the two off-duty nurses, Hannah Briggs and Gerry Campbell, who were coming in the mini-bus to help with the residents. Ruth the other maid, and her husband Arthur Taylor, also appeared in unnaturally smart outfits. They all stood around, saying little and feeling a lot in their hearts. Even Aggie Brown was quiet. Amy felt the tears beginning, and turned to Arthur on the pretext of making sure they had enough petrol. The two of them left the room, and the others began coming out, to be helped up the ramp and into their seats.

The sun blazed down, giving of its best as they made their way along the winding country road to the village of Daweswater, to say goodbye to their best friend. The stone cottages looked radiant, their faces covered with roses and honeysuckle. The little church was glorious in its sunlight, the whitewashed stone reflecting the light as a human reflection of the Kingdom of Heaven. The altar held a silver cross, and two small bowls of white roses. The church was empty but for Canon Forrester. He had asked Amy to be early, before the other villagers took their seats.

The front pew was left for Dr Mac's family—although Amy privately thought that the Manor people were closer to him than his blood relations, whom they had never seen. She knew his wife had died a long time ago, that there had been a second wife briefly. But the staff at the Manor had mothered him more, and he had not seemed to notice that he had no family with him.

The organist was playing Bach. The Canon came and shook hands with them all. 'You do suppose Dr MacFarlane will get here on time?' he asked Amy.

'I gave him the time over the phone.' And at that moment they heard car engines at the door, and the Canon went to welcome the relatives. The churchwarden showed villagers to the last seats, and went to the school hall for more chairs. Amy tried not to look round. She would meet Dr MacFarlane later at the buffet—for the first and last time, she hoped.

The doors suddenly opened wider, and the organist began to play more softly, as Canon Forrester's well-known voice was heard reciting the familiar words as he preceded the coffin to the altar . . . 'I am the Resurrection and the Life, saith the Lord: he that believeth in me, though he were dead, yet shall he live. . . .'

A tall man and a blue-rinsed woman walked next. The

entire congregation tried not to stare, and failed miser-
ably. What a man! His eyes were a clear blue, the colour
of the summer sky, his chin and mouth and nose were
sculptured to perfection, firm yet not brutal. His hair
was curly, neatly cut but boyishly unruly around his ears
and at his nape—Amy thought she had never seen a
more noble and handsome back of anyone's head in
her life. The adjective 'Greek' sprang to mind. And she
bent her own head, ashamed of her natural feminine
response.

The woman must be his stepmother. She was expens-
ively dressed, and her scrap of black net must have cost a
lot more than Amy's little straw. She was solemnly
gazing at the Canon, subdued but not grief-stricken. It
was impossible to read the sky-blue eyes of the man at
her side.

Behind them came a loose-lipped youth in rather
trendy clothes, the trousers baggy and the jacket too
large on the shoulders. And beside him was a lovely dark
woman—Italian maybe, or possibly Spanish or Cypriot.
Her hair hung in a glossy bob, giving off highlights as she
swung her head to find her prayer-book. Amy straightened her country straw hat and concentrated on the
service.

After the service, as Amy stood at the graveside,
unashamedly crying, unwilling to leave her dear friend,
she saw that the tall man also had stayed behind. He
looked across the pile of earth loosely covering the oak
coffin, and said softly, 'I'm Chris—we spoke on the
telephone. You're Amy Taggart, aren't you?'

'Yes.' She tried to control her voice, and as he took a
stride to get round to her side of the grave, she added,
'How do you do? I'm sorry we had to meet so sadly. He
was a father to all of us at Greyrigg, you know.'

'He was?' Chris MacFarlane didn't sound all that
interested. Amy felt annoyed with him for not showing
more emotion. 'Let's go and see the famous Greyrigg
Manor, then. I never actually got round to visiting it
when I came up to see my father.'

Amy led the way, feeling protective towards the Manor. 'You mustn't make any snap judgements about the Manor. It may not seem wonderful at first sight, but when you get to know it, you'll know what I mean.'

'Some things around here do appear wonderful at first sight.' And the look in those very direct eyes were almost insolent as he stared at her. She felt embarrassed as he took in with that raking look her silk blouse, her little hat, her simple suit. What an awful man! Could she really feel confident that he would appreciate the atmosphere at the Manor? It seemed very unlikely. Yet he was Dr Mac's son; there must be something good in him. She would give him the rest of the day to show it before she disliked him completely.

They walked round to the front of the church together without speaking. 'Let me take you in my car,' Chris MacFarlane offered. 'Your lot have gone off without you.'

'It isn't far to walk.'

'Please. I don't know the way.'

His droopy friend was getting into a dark green Jaguar with the pretty girl, the blue-haired woman was shooting off round the corner in a pale blue Lancia, and Chris was opening the door of a sleek white BMW. Amy got in very selfconsciously. He seated himself beside her and fastened the belt, saying casually, 'The fair chap is my bosom friend Quintin. Don't be misled by his dopey look—he's a clever fellow. The girl is Indian—her name is Sharla and she's a superb physiotherapist. I wasn't sure what facilities you have here, but I'm sure she'll be a great asset.' And as he started the car and purred around the corner, Amy's worst fears were coming true. He was going to change their routine; he was going to modernise the Manor! She folded her arms across her chest and held her arms tightly, restraining herself from saying anything. Chris remarked, 'You're very quiet, Amy Taggart.'

'Don't worry. I'm probably leaving soon, so there isn't any need to explain any more.'

'Leaving? Why didn't you mention this to me over the phone?'

'I only decided recently,' she told him.

He looked amused. 'Like right now, Amy? That's what it looks like to me.' And when she didn't answer, he said, 'I hope you aren't thinking of going and leaving everyone in the lurch? I understood you to be very conscientious and well thought of.'

She said without looking at him, 'I won't do anything hastily. Turn left here.'

They passed the tattered old sign. Chris said nothing, but as he steered carefully up the drive he stole a sideways look at Amy, and she knew he sensed her resentment and her fierce pride in Greyrigg Manor, in what they had built up together. She didn't see the expression in the blue eyes as he said quietly, 'It's a lovely old place, Amy—beautiful. I think I know what you meant—it needs a bit of tidying up. But the façade is delightful. I see Quintin thinks so too.' And as they got out of the car, they saw Quintin already taking photographs with an expensive-looking camera. Chris said, 'Amy, this is Quintin Forbes—he's something of an architect and interior designer. Might be useful to us, don't you think?'

Amy shook hands with Quintin and wished she were a witch and could make him and Christopher MacFarlane together disappear for ever, or turn into frogs.

'And this is Sharla Chowdray. I know you two are going to get on.'

Sharla smiled at Amy as they shook hands. Amy was surprised to see warmth and genuine interest in those lovely dark brown eyes. 'Hello, Amy. You are so lucky to live in a place like this. I've never seen anything so lovely since I left Kashmir.'

That was better. Still, Sharla too wasn't needed. But Amy was slightly more effusive towards her. 'It's nice to meet you. Come in and meet our residents. They all want to tell you how they loved Dr Mac.'

Faith Hindle was something of a vamp in her own

small way. She came up to Amy after all the introductions had been made, and hissed in her ear, 'I'd try out his bedside manner any day!'

Amy turned with pursed lips. 'Go and help Ruth with the sandwiches. And tell Gwyn we need a few more small plates for the cakes.' She saw Chris MacFarlane across the room, making himself charming to Arthur Taylor. He was taller than most men in the room. And his eyes seemed to mesmerise her, piercing the atmosphere of polite conversation to reveal more basic emotions beneath the veneer of respectability. He turned as though expecting her to be staring, and gave her a secret one-sided smile, before turning back with feigned interest in what Arthur was saying.

This was awful! The man could read her very thoughts. And to make matters worse, she couldn't hide her admiration for him, and he knew it too. There was nothing she could do except try not to look in his direction, and hope he went home soon.

The blue-rinsed lady walked over with an air of being very used to mixing at parties. 'You must be Amy. How do you do, my dear? I do compliment you on the wonderful organisation here. I'm Veronica Standish, ex-Mrs MacFarlane. I thought the world of dear Roderick, of course—everyone did—but I just couldn't bear life away from town.'

'I see.' Amy and Dr Mac had talked little of his private life. 'I can see that life out here wouldn't suit everyone. It's nice of you to come all this way.'

'As I said, I was fond of Roderick. And also I wanted another look at Four Winds—our house on Kilderbarrow, you know, just outside Keswick.'

'I've never seen it,' said Amy. 'Dr Mac stayed here most of the time.'

'I'm not even sure who it belongs to. Possibly Chris. But I'll take a trip over before I go. And who is this nice young man?' Mrs Standish looked up as a tall fair figure joined their group.

Amy smiled up at Larry Ford. 'This is our GP, Mrs

Standish. He and Cyril Oxenholme look after our patients when Dr Mac isn't here—wasn't here . . .' It would take some time to get used to his absence. Larry shook hands with the elegant Mrs Standish, and exchanged a few polite nothings for a while. Then he turned to Amy as Veronica drifted on to another group. 'You must be feeling pretty rotten. But he wasn't a well man, you know—his chest was in a very dicey state. I blame that pipe of his.'

'It was his time to go, I suppose.' Amy sighed, knowing she could be natural with Larry. They weren't exactly going out together, but they had spent a few evenings at the cinema, and they saw most of the Century Theatre productions down by Lake Derwentwater. 'I'm afraid you're the one to suffer too, Larry. You'll get an awful lot more calls than you're used to.'

Chris MacFarlane passed them, on his way to shake Gwyn Jones by the hand, and thank her for the buffet. Larry said, 'Typical arrogant consultant, I suppose. But I like this girl-friend Sharla. She's friendly—and she's gorgeous.'

Amy smiled. 'You won't mind extra calls out here, then. Sharla is staying on as resident physiotherapist.'

Larry's face brightened. 'Somehow I don't think I will!' He turned towards the rest of the room. 'Have you introduced young Christopher to the residents yet?'

But there was no need. Major Charles Hendon had collared him. Leaning heavily on his stick, but his head militarily erect as always, he introduced himself, and Aggie Brown and Sarah-Jane Phelps in her wheelchair. 'Your father usually needed a little help with the *Times* crossword,' the Major said, shaking hands with Chris.

Amy listened, while trying not to look. Chris MacFarlane was a model of etiquette. He listened courteously to the Major, exchanged some kindly words with Aggie, and expressed great surprise that Sarah-Jane was nearly a hundred years old. At first sight, she knew he was making an excellent impression. But Larry Ford had seen through him. An arrogant consultant.

Aggie Brown wasted no time. 'It's not the same without Dr Mac. Are you coming to stay with us, then, lad?'

'Afraid not, Aggie—far too much work with my practice. But I'll be here if you need me, never fear.' His smile was ready and looked genuine, and the old lady smiled back, charmed.

Chris worked his way round the residents, shaking hands and assuring them that he wanted the Manor to stay as happy as it obviously was. Amy wondered if it was time to relax. Maybe she had been too apprehensive. A new physio department wouldn't come amiss, and Sharla Chowdray seemed an admirable addition to the staff.

The guests were satisfied, and Gwyn and her helpers began to clear away. Olive and Gerry began to see their charges indoors for an afternoon rest—they had been wandering through the french windows and round the garden, almost like a garden party except for the sad memories they all held in their hearts. Chris was still active in the public relations department. 'Well done, Lucy! I look forward to hearing you play.' Lucy Coats was their blind lady, an ex-music teacher and pianist. He helped Flo and Damaris, two old friends who stuck together and looked after each other, into the room, where Olive took them over. And he even bent and kissed Sarah-Jane's hand as she was wheeled in, an act which ensured her eternal devotion.

'You must come to my party—February the fourteenth. A hundred years old, Dr Mac. You don't mind me calling you that?'

'I'm honoured, Miss Phelps.'

He looked up then, and caught Amy's expression. He made a few more farewells and she turned away, disgusted by his easy manner, which she considered totally false. She walked across to Graham and Edna Bell, their married couple who had come from Oxford, where Edna had been a Professor of Philosophy and Graham a senior don. 'You've met Dr MacFarlane, Edna?'

'Yes indeed, thank you, Amy. What a cultured gentleman!' Amy held out her arm for Edna and Graham to help each other up, and the threesome walked indoors together. Martha Quayle and Doris Owens were sitting together in the dining room, and Amy left the Bells with them, as she went back to the garden to check that no-one had been left behind.

In the distance she could hear Aggie taunting Sarah-Jane—a common occurrence. 'Don't believe her, Dr Mac. She's making it up. No one's seen her birth certificate.'

'You nasty little tittle-tattle!' Ninety-nine or not, Sarah-Jane had a good line in invective. 'Just wait till you get to my age! You'll wish you had more respect for your elders.'

'Well, Amy?' She knew it was Chris without looking. He was smiling down at her and they were hidden from the house by a large yew. 'Do I get a gold star for good behaviour?'

'I'm sorry if some of them were—a bit forward, sir. They don't mean it. It isn't disrespect, it's affection,' Amy assured him.

Chris MacFarlane put out his hand and touched her shoulder, and she tried not to shiver at his unexpected closeness. 'Amy Taggart, take off that ridiculous hat. And don't ever call me sir again!'

She obeyed him, angry at his amused look, at the way he gave orders, and he smiled. 'That's better. You have the prettiest hair in the world. What do we do now, Amy?'

'I'm going to help the others clear up. You're welcome to stay—after all, it does belong to you.' She hoped this was the moment she could say goodbye to this pushy young physician from London.

'You'll have to stay and entertain me, Amy—after all, we have a great deal to talk about. I'm staying at the Meridien for another night, so we can cover all the topics I've got listed here.' He took a paper from the top pocket of his neat dark grey suit. She turned to him, resigned, and he took her elbow. 'Let's sit under this tree. And you don't mind if I take off my jacket, do you?'

She caught sight of some of the items on his list, written in neat black handwriting. Top was the physiotherapy unit; next was redecoration and repairs. She sat down on the bench under the willow tree and folded her hands together, ready to fight for Greyrigg Manor as she knew it. 'I'm ready,' she said. She laid her hat on the bench beside her. Chris picked it up so that he could sit closer to her, and hung it ridiculously from a willow branch.

'Right,' he said, rolling up his sleeves. 'You do know that I've installed Quintin in Dad's room?' Her face said enough. He went on, 'I want him to undertake a thorough survey of the Manor, noting all defects and repairs. After that, I've asked him to design it according to some rules of my own, with extra ramps and maybe a few less doors. He should take about two months.'

Modernisation, then. Reorganisation. All she had feared. As far as Amy was concerned he was totally destroying the Manor, totally destroying the life they had lived there for years. She said without looking at him, 'This is all decided, is it? You don't want to discuss anything with me—just give me an ultimatum?'

He turned towards her, so that his knee brushed against hers. 'Not a bit. I want to discuss all of it. After all, you did say you might be leaving, so I really have to have an in-depth talk about the way everything is run, so that I know how to carry on without you.' She met his gaze then, and was struck again by the blue eyes, the penetrating look that she was sure gave him a good bedside manner for his female patients. Yet they were sincere and honest too, making men trust and like him. As their eyes met, he gave a little smile, as though gratified by her facing him, and gave her hair a little ruffle of—was it affection? She tried not to shrink away from him, and felt her cheeks growing hot. 'I do hope you don't leave me in the lurch. But then I know you won't, Amy. Everyone talks of your devotion to your

patients. You wouldn't leave them unless you knew
someone good was taking over, right?'

'Yes, of course.' She had to make that clear. 'Who else
do they have, now that Dr Mac is gone?'

'They have me.'

'And how often will you want to be bothered by their
little requests, their petty problems? I can just see you
leaving your posh rooms to take a phone call about
Damaris Jarvis's phlebitis!'

Chris stood up, and wandered to a gap in the trees
where he could see the lake. 'It's no use pretending I'm
Dad. How can I be? I was encouraged to specialise
young, to be a whizz-kid and pass every exam in sight. I
had the brains—Dad had the connections—all the right
jobs fell into my lap. I can't leave my practice now.
Anyway, I'd get bored stiff here—all this deadly peace
and quiet! I'd miss London life. It's good.'

'Quiet?' Amy echoed. 'You mean you can't hear
the skylark? And the sheep calling their lambs? And
the beck coming down the fellside behind the Manor
gardens?'

He looked at her, and turned back to the view,
listening now. 'Oh yes, I hear.' He walked back to her.
'You must find us all a bit flash, Amy Taggart, us city
types.' He was teasing her, but in a nice way.

Just then Quintin Forbes came bounding round the
bushes. 'Oh, there you are, Chris. Word with you, old
man. This place has terrific possibilities—it speaks to
me. Reminds me of Pinky Potter's place in Devon, you
remember? I had a whale of a time there. Archways all
through, the crimson room, the conservatory lights . . .'

Amy stood up. 'If you don't need me . . .'

Chris said, 'All right, if you have things to do. I'll catch
up with you in a moment.' She left them talking quietly,
her heart heavy. What was this madman going to do to
Greyrigg? And how long could she stay and see it
ruined?

She went indoors and helped with the washing up.
Sharla Chowdray came in, and seeing everyone busy,

picked up a towel and helped them with the dishes. Amy smiled. 'You must like hard work,' she remarked.

'I don't mind it.' Sharla's gentle eyes clouded for a moment, and she hesitated in what she was doing. Then she squared her shoulders and carried on. Amy said no more; she would confide in her when she felt she knew her well enough. Sharla said after a moment, 'I like your old people, Amy. And I love this place very much. It reminds me a little bit of Kashmir.'

Sharla was nice. One out of three wasn't bad. But Chris was too arrogant for his own good, and Quintin was insufferable . . . Amy caught her breath as Chris came in through the back door. 'Amy, I'll call for you at seven to discusss things over dinner!'

CHAPTER TWO

AMY took some trouble over her appearance. Dinner at the Meridien was not just any old dinner—even though it was a working meal, and she assumed Sharla and Quintin would be there too. She was apprehensive, but determined to stand up for non-intervention in the way Greyrigg Manor was run. This evening could be crucial. And she had to be firm with the insolent young man who was Dr Mac's only son—without antagonising him, if at all possible. A working relationship, that enabled him to get back to his London practice without interfering in their formerly ordered and contented lives.

She stood in front of the mirror, trying to decide which of her two best dresses would impress a handsome Harley Street physician. The evening air was sweet through her open windows, warm and sensuous. It had already been a tiring day, and it would have been perfect just to sit beside Lucy Coats, as she played some gentle Chopin nocturnes from her prodigious memory, her blind eyes closed as she played, or sit with Flo and Damaris under the yew tree, and talk of old times, times when Amy's grandfather used to farm on the other side of the lake, and her father as well before his illness . . .

She decided on a cotton voile dress in pale lemon with cap sleeves. It was pretty and cool. She could have wished she looked older and more sophisticated. However, young Dr Mac was going to find out anyway that she had an old head on young shoulders.

She brushed out her brown curly hair, recalling with a rueful grimace the way Chris had dared to ruffle it when she removed her hat that afternoon—on his instructions. There must be none of that tonight. She must be mistress of herself, drink no wine that might fuddle her thinking, accept no compliments, not allow the conversation to wander from the original agenda. Amy pulled out from inside the wardrobe her only pair of high-heeled sandals. She tried them on, stretching out her sunburnt legs to admire the sudden elegance they gave her. Yes, she was ready now. Feeling good would give her that extra confidence to speak her mind to the new—and unwelcome—Dr Mac.

She knew the white BMW was there at the door as she ran down the stairs. She could hear the engine running, cool and sophisticated as the owner, a rich and expensive sound. And there was Chris himself, just coming in, framed in the doorway by green yew and roses, dressed in tailored white silk shirt and dark grey slacks that showed off his casual elegance. The scent of the roses followed him in. 'Well, Sister Taggart, you're ready on the dot. Wonderful you look too!' He looked down at her with that keen stare. Was it admiration in his blue eyes, or was he sizing her up, wondering how to get her in a pliant mood so that she would not object to his far-reaching ideas about the Manor?

'Yes, Dr MacFarlane.' She looked down modestly, giving nothing away. It sounded wrong for this clever young upstart to have the same name as darling silver-headed Dr Mac, the man who had breathed the very soul into Greyrigg in his gruff but golden-hearted way. What could Chris have to offer them, apart from disruption and change? Clever he undoubtedly was, but he could never match his father for gentleness, for caring . . .

'Shall we go?' he said.

'Where are the others?'

'There are no others, Amy.' His voice was brisk, businesslike, already sounding as though he was organising her. He took her arm, his fingers hard as steel on her bare flesh. 'Now, I thought we'd sit by the pool for half an hour, watch the sun go down behind Kilderbarrow, while you tell me all about your life here.'

Amy sat down in the front seat, and he closed the door gently. She closed her eyes briefly, telling herself urgently that he mustn't be allowed to stay in the driving

seat when it came to conversation. But as he sat beside
her, she noticed his perfect pectoral muscles when he
fastened his seat belt, and had to look out of the window
to control her thoughts. Then she smiled, seeing Aggie
Brown at the window. Aggie was checking up on her.
She waved a jaunty hand, and put up one thumb.

'What does that mean?' asked Chris. 'A secret signal?'

'In a way.'

'What?'

'It wouldn't be secret if I told you,' smiled Amy.

'Oh, so that's the way! Non-co-operation already?'

Amy allowed herself to face him as he drove round the
still, peaceful lake. The shadows of the fells were deeply
reflected in the glassy surface and the sky was sheer and
luminous. She was going to argue with him, to protest
that co-operation had to be impartial, but the sheer
beauty of the silent evening took away any aggressive
thoughts for a while. Chris said, 'Go on. You were going
to tick me off.'

She was able to feel just slightly superior. 'You're a
city man, you can't ever know the lake as I do. In this
mood, I could stay with it for hours and say nothing.
Words are just not necessary.'

Chris said nothing, but as they crossed the stone
bridge across the river at the end of the lake, he steered
the car into a small layby, with a view of the Manor
across the still water. 'You don't mind if we stop for a
moment? It seems strange that on the day I see my father
buried, my mind can be so at peace. I didn't know him
well—but from what I've heard today, I can't help
feeling he's trying to tell me something.' And Amy saw
with surprise that he looked embarrassed at the admission. Perhaps he wasn't used to being so frank.
Perhaps it wasn't the fashion in his crowd.

For a moment she saw only a man who had lost his
father. 'Why don't you get out?' she suggested. She
knew from a lifetime's experience the medicinal effect of
the lakes and the heather and the bracken and the fells.
And she also knew that the more time he spent in the

midst of this glory, the more he would understand his father.

He obeyed her, standing with his hands deep in his pockets. Managing to ignore his obvious charm, his physical strength and beauty, she looked past him to the distant peaks, clear against the sky, the vivid purple of the heather splashing in abandon across the grey rocks. No painter in the world could capture the way the fading light transfigured the surface of the water. But Amy was quite used to the way the sheer intensity of beauty made her want to cry.

As Chris returned to the car, she saw that he had experienced it too. He sat down and reached for his belt. A little group of brown ducks emerged quacking from a small bay and swam cheekily across the panorama, spreading ripples as they paddled. He turned and said, 'Just look at that! When you have something perfect, someone always comes along and makes waves.' There was no disguising the fact that he was referring to the Manor. Was he saying that the waves that were made were purely temporary, that the same picture was there, unaffected basically by the waves? In fact, the little ripples added to the total picture. Amy looked down, knowing herself unqualified to argue with him. She gripped the sides of the seat with her fingers, praying that his mastery of her would not extend to their discussions later.

They turned into the Meridien drive. A doorman appeared immediately and Chris gave him the car keys and left him to park the car, while they strolled casually across tailored lawns towards the outdoor pool, surrounded by small tables and striped umbrellas. For a country hotel, the Meridien was out of place, catering as it did for foreign diplomats, for parents who always brought a nanny, for sheer affluence. It was almost continental. Amy decided it suited Chris. But old Dr Mac had never been here, preferring the gentle atmosphere of the local Pheasant with its oak beams, good ale and its rooks in the tall elms in the garden.

They found a table by the pool. Most of the children were being taken away by their nannies. The pool's ripples slowly subsided, leaving the blue-green water still and decorative under the spotlights that were just coming on as dusk fell. 'Glass of wine, Amy?' asked Chris.

One glass could do no harm. 'Chablis, please.'

She knew that Chris was eyeing her, trying to make her out. She was selfconscious under the intense study, but tried not to show it. Those blue eyes of his were powerful, revealing a powerful nature. But the Taggart determination, though dented, was certainly not breached. She looked out across the greying horizon and pretended Chris MacFarlane was just another ordinary man . . .

The last rays of the sun were warm, comfortable. They reached the tips of the fells, and any moment would bring the sudden loss of light. The scarlet geraniums in the hotel windowboxes were startling in their vividness, brilliant against the cool grey-green stone. The waiter brought a shiny pail on legs, and withdrew a dark green bottle, poured refreshing wine into crystal glasses, before replacing it with a crunch among the ice. Chris said, as he held up his glass with the late sunlight refracted through it, 'To Greyrigg, Amy.' His voice was cool, businesslike. 'Let's hope the transition isn't too painful.'

She had to look at him to respond. Looking straight into his devastating eyes, she said, 'Greyrigg Manor, and all who live there.' Perhaps Chris didn't care too much about them. But he was going to, if it were humanly possible. Amy waited, letting Chris make the next move.

He said, in studied casualness, 'I want to apologise for landing Quint and Sharla on you so suddenly. I know I should have discussed it with you first, but I'm hellishly busy in the practice, and this was the best opportunity to get them installed. I wouldn't be able to get away for at least another month, and that would have been a wasted month.' He spoke politely, but his tone implied that she ought to respect a busy man such as he, and make allowances. Amy said nothing, and Chris said, irritated, 'Well?'

Amy was distant. 'You obviously have everything planned out. Why bother to bring me here? That was perfectly obvious from the start.'

'Oh, for God's sake! I thought I might get a bit of sense out of you.' Chris apparently suddenly remembered that this was a public relations exercise. 'Sorry, I didn't miscalculate, did I, Amy? You are dedicated to the welfare of the Manor?'

'You know that. And devoted to Dr Mac.'

'He did tell me. I didn't visit often, but I'd heard about you.'

The shadows lengthened, the last rays of the sun catching the geraniums and the green ivy on the hotel walls. A small blonde child ran down to the pool, given permission by its nanny for one last length. One could sympathise. The evening was too warm and lovely to have to go to bed. As she giggled in the twilight, the child was caught in a big towel, hugged and taken back. The ripples shimmered in the light from the windows as the sun disappeared—and she knew why. This tall and very confident young man was devilishly attractive, and he also presented the threat of a whole range of new ideas that she didn't want to hear.

'What are you thinking, Amy?'

She took a deep breath. 'A lot of small matters that don't need to trouble you. Miss Phelps' birth certificate for one. She can't prove she's a hundred next February —and without that certificate she won't get a telegram from the Queen.'

'That's a tough one.' He was mocking, of course.

'I'm sorry, but to our guests, these are serious and knotty problems. You're a high-flier compared with us here, Chris. You've no idea how a community works, how we learn to give and take, to build up a haven where it's pleasant and comfortable to be.'

Chris held out his hands in a gesture of self-protection.

'I acknowledge my ignorance, my lord. Go on, tell me all about it. That's what I want to know. Show me how Dad made it work.'

'You wouldn't understand,' Amy shrugged.

His tone hardened. 'That's a rather unkind response, Amy. I've just been handed a sheaf of bills—my responsibility now. I don't think it's unreasonable to want to hear how things work, how necessary these bills are. You probably think that someone who knows how to run things economically has no heart, but the two things aren't incompatible, you know. If you call yourself a manager, then show me how you manage, Amy Taggart.'

'If you don't want me, I'm quite happy to resign.' Her voice was as hard as his.

'Don't be so touchy, woman! You can't resign yet. It wouldn't be fair on your guests, leaving them to someone who doesn't know them.' Even when angry, Chris had an extraordinary attractiveness, the eyebrows straight over those clear eyes, the chin aggressively firm. 'For goodness' sake . . .'

The waiter appeared to pour a second glass of wine, and hostilities ceased in an embarrassed silence. Over the lake a curlew cried, and was answered by another. Amy sipped her wine in an effort to take hold of herself. Why were they both so heated? Surely they were rational people, who could talk without shouting, even though their ideas were miles apart.

Chris said to the waiter as he replaced the bottle in the melting ice, 'Does the hotel have a boat?'

'No, sir. But the jetty down there among the trees has some rowing boats for hire.' He withdrew, with a knowing glance at the faces of the combatants.

Amy asked, 'What do you want a boat for?'

'I like sailing.'

'In that case, I have a GP in the boathouse across there.' She pointed across the sleek surface of the lake, where a few twinkling lights showed up Daweswater village, and the Manor farther along. 'If you have time, I can take you out in the morning.'

'Your own General Purpose? Wonderful! What time can I come?'

'Nineish.' The atmosphere had thawed considerably. 'You sail well?' Amy asked.

'I've been at it since I was eleven.'

The menus were brought out to them, but Chris waved them away. 'We'll start with papaya and mango, then the roast partridge with quails' eggs and asparagus. Amy, sautéed potatoes?'

'Yes.' Back at the Manor, supper was sardine salad. But she would have preferred to be there, where the lettuce was straight out of the garden, the whole-meal bread home-baked, and the company restful and familiar.

Other couples came down to the pool, already dressed for dinner, and the coloured floodlights came on with a flash, making Amy blink as she saw the handsome face of her companion in stark clarity. He stood up. 'Let's go in.' They crossed the lawn again, and paused at its edge, looking out across the still water, the sound of humming midges in the trees, and chirping crickets. And then as they took a step nearer, they saw the full moon, breath-takingly reflected in the dark blue water. There was no breath of wind. Chris said softly, 'How sweet the moon-light sleeps upon this bank.'

It was Shakespeare. Amy went on, 'Here will we sit, and let the sound of music creep in our ears. Soft stillness and the night become the touches of sweet harmony.'

Chris turned to face her, a smile making his face suddenly appealingly boyish. 'On such a night as this . . . did Amy Taggart decide that Christopher MacFarlane wasn't some sort of bogeyman?' His voice was very soft, lingering over the words as he pulled her closer towards him. 'Agreed, Amy?' She didn't reply, affected sud-denly by his magnetic maleness. She could feel her heart fluttering behind her ribs, and felt a sense of fury and helplessness, that she could no longer control her own

reactions. How could she talk business with her
breathing going all peculiar?

They entered the dining room, a luxurious salon, all
the windows open in the extraordinary heatwave, and
palm trees in pots waving in the swirling fans in the
ceiling. Amy thought people would imagine them to be
close friends, the way Chris steered her to his table, his
arm gently round her shoulders as though he cared for
her . . . as though she were precious to him.

He began to talk, quite naturally, and the waiter
poured yet more wine. 'I knew the old man wouldn't go
on for ever. But somehow I wasn't prepared to take over
so suddenly. It's a responsibility, all right, the Manor.
But I do intend to do what's right. I'd like to think that
when I decide to leave, people will have some good
things to say about me.'

'You mean you might sell?' Amy's heart fluttered
even more.

'Possibly. But I'd like to try and make a go of it. If
you'll help me?'

'Naturally I hope you will. But you don't need
Quintin. He wants to make alterations without seeing
Greyrigg in winter. We must have our doors, properly
fitting too. Archways would be ridiculous. How can he
possibly make any decisions without seeing how the
residents live in the cold weather?'

'I suppose the bills are high in winter?'

'Well, of course they are. Dr Mac never said a word
about them. He knew we did our best, and electricity
isn't cheap.' Amy despised the way Chris saw life in
monetary terms. 'You'd hate it—snow and ice and
blocked roads and extra blankets.'

'Are you inviting me to be absent? I'd like to see how
you cope!'

'I thought Quintin was your spy?'

'That isn't fair.' His eyes were stern under straight
brows again. 'A spy is unknown—you can all see and
hear Quintin, and I make no secret of what he's doing.
After all, he can improve the place as well as alter it.

What about the roof insulation? I bet they didn't know about fibreglass when the Manor was built.'

'I suppose we might need insulation,' Amy agreed. 'Lizzie Black feels the cold terribly, and Becky Davis and George Bridges. Becky's arthritis is always bad in winter.'

'George is the one with cancer?'

'How did you know?' Chris had only shaken hands with him once, exchanged a couple of words.

'No flesh on him. He won't make it till next summer.'

'The operation was successful—bowel cancer. They said he had a chance.'

'The gut isn't working properly. Probably ischaemia.' Chris shook his head. 'He won't make it, Amy.' He finished his mango, and looked at her as she pushed hers to one side. 'The Major needs hip surgery, doesn't he? And I noticed that Damaris—she's the tiny pretty woman, isn't she?—she has Reynaud's phenomenon even in midsummer. The tips of her forefingers were both white.' He gave what Amy thought was a superior smile. 'You see, you do need Quintin. He'll recommend improvements you really need. Trust him, Amy.'

Amy refused the sweet trolley. It had been a rich and splendid meal. They finished with a slice of Stilton cheese and a glass of port. She had enjoyed the luxury, but was angry at the way Chris spent so much money on a meal, yet quibbled about the housekeeping at Greyrigg, where no one was very extravagant. He wanted her to be some sort of heartless accounting machine, meeting the budget, but not the needs of the residents.

They strolled in the garden afterwards. 'Tell me what you're thinking,' Chris invited.

'That you don't really need me.' Amy was reluctant to say it, but she felt it was true. 'You want someone who puts profit first.'

'That's untrue and unkind!' he snapped at her, the mellowness of the meal vanishing immediately. They walked in silence for a while, each concerned with their own thoughts. Then Chris said as though to himself,

'I've tried to explain my attitude. Somehow you seem to have taken a dislike to anything I say. That's called prejudice.'

Amy pressed her lips together, wishing she could hit him. 'Have you said all you wanted to say?'

He looked across the lake to the opposite shore, to the dark fells rising up, blotting out the stars. 'Somehow I know we can be friends. Maybe not now—but I do need you, Amy, to supervise everything, to keep an eye on Quint, to keep me posted about the way things are going. Write regularly, and phone every week, please.'

Amy said sourly, 'We mustn't be uneconomical. I'll write, it's cheaper.'

Chris swung round and seized her shoulders, crushing the tiny cap sleeves of the lemon voile. 'You infuriating woman!' But as she looked up, facing him with grim determination, his voice suddenly changed. 'And so very pretty, so terribly pretty.' A million fancies danced in her mind. She felt suddenly hot and a little afraid. He took his hands away from her sleeves, and she knew there must be marks where his strong fingers had gripped. Then he caught her into his arms, pulled her roughly against his chest, and held her for a moment. When she didn't pull away, he bent and kissed her expertly, taking her lips gently with his, then increasing the pressure as the feeling became sweeter and more exciting. The moment vanished into eternity, the lake and the hotel disappeared, and she knew nothing but total sweetness and total surrender. The attraction which had first made her blush in church that morning had shown itself openly now, and she could never pretend that he meant nothing to her, ever again.

He let her go, and they walked again, his arm around her shoulders. In a low voice he said, 'What are you thinking now?'

'That I had too much wine and made a fool of myself.'

'No, no, Amy, it wasn't like that,' he assured her.

'I came hoping for your respect——' Amy began.

'You have it.'

'Oh no, I haven't. You think I'm pretty and pre-judiced. But what I really hoped for I haven't got.'

Chris stopped and made her face him again. 'Neither have I. But there's always tomorrow. It is still on, is it, that invitation to sail?'

'Of course.' At least grappling with the wind, they could call a truce to their differences. 'I'd better go now.'

There was so much she hadn't found out—about his mother, about his practice, about his early days with Dr Mac, and what he thought about his father. But that kiss had stopped all natural conversation, and the emotion she had felt was still making her thoughts whirl and dance out of control.

He stopped at the gates of the drive. 'The engine might disturb your residents,' he explained, but he was quick to come round and open the door of the car for her. 'Good night, Amy Taggart.'

Her voice was a trifle husky as she murmured a good night, then turned and walked very fast away from him. She hadn't thanked him. What for? It was just about the most disturbing evening she had ever spent, in spite of the peace of the surroundings. An owl hooted derisively in the yew, she looked up, and found herself smiling at its cheek. 'And to you,' she replied, as she let herself in. She stood by the door, listening as Chris's car retraced the road through Daweswater village, past Mr Gately's shop, past the whitewashed church, and the new grave . . .

She looked around the dark hall, lit only by the moonlight. How dared he come here and try to change things? Greyrigg had been like this since any of them could remember. It would be cruel and unnecessary surgery to try to change its character, to run it in any other way. On the way upstairs, she felt the warmth and the comfort of ages of friendly ghosts. Dr Mac was here too. He would help them as he always had.

She was woken by the rooster at Thorn Howe Farm, just up the road. That was where they brought their eggs, their goats' milk and damsons. Amy opened her eyes, knowing that things were different, that she would never go back to that gentle routine they had known for so many years. One half of her insisted on being exhilarated by the excitement that was Chris MacFarlane; the other half was pessimistic about what was going to happen, now that Chris's London cronies had got a toehold at the Manor.

She jumped up, flung on her shirt and shorts, and whistled to Nell, who was always stationed at the door, ready for their morning run. The dew was fresh and welcome on their legs, the gentle mist fading imperceptibly away as the sun grew stronger. Yet another perfect day—weatherwise if nothing else. The lake looked very inviting, and she ran even faster as she thought of getting *Speedwell* out and catching at the light breeze that played among the lush leaves. Nell ran rings about her, and barked for sticks to be thrown.

'Nice young man, eh?'

'Who do you mean, Mr Gately?' Amy knew very well, but tried to distance herself from any warm feelings for Chris MacFarlane.

Mr Gately knew she knew. 'Civil he was, and pleasant. Nice-looking head on his shoulders too. Staying long?'

'He goes back today.'

'When's he coming back?'

'Time will tell.' Amy wanted to criticise Chris, but somehow the words wouldn't come. 'I can't really see him spending much of his valuable time with us country bumpkins.'

'Oho!' Mr Gately piled the newspapers into her usual bunch, and smiled to himself. 'That's how it is, is it?' And Amy felt herself blushing as she turned and made her way back, kicking at the grass to make the dew scatter in clouds of mist.

Billy Braithwaite was on his way to the town. 'Ee, lass, it's nearly dinner time. I beat you by an hour,' he grinned.

Amy excused herself. 'Late night.'

'Aye, I 'eard,' Billy laughed as he revved up the old engine, and Amy blushed yet again. All the same, the sun was warm, the birds were singing their hearts out, and the campers were beginning to crawl out of their caravans and tents and reach for their big boots and rucksacks.

Amy breakfasted quickly, then went to see that all was well with the residents. Hannah Briggs was on duty, with her usual brisk no-nonsense approach and her large heart. Gerry Campbell was in charge of the men, though Hannah always finished first, in spite of the fact that there were fourteen women and only four men. Gerry was pushing the wheelchair along for William O'Hara as Amy came in. 'Everything all right?' asked Amy.

'Sure. Nice day again, Amy.'

'I'm going down to the boathouse. If you need me, give me a whistle. I won't go far out.'

'Take your time. I've got the whistle.'

Amy went down the road, and through the kissing gate that led down to the lake. *Speedwell* lay welcoming, her sail neatly rolled and covered with a sheet of polythene. Nell had followed Amy, and now frisked around her, knowing she was to get a sail, which she loved. 'Take it easy, Able Seaman,' joked Amy, as Nell jumped up and licked her face. She felt a trifle nervous of seeing Chris again in the full glare of the morning. But she had resolved not to argue with him. Neither of them could give in. So let them enjoy the breeze, and forget their differences for an hour.

When the cracking of dry sticks on the lakeside path alerted her to Chris's arrival, she felt again the quickening of her heartbeats. She tried to think of something clever to say, but her mouth felt dry, and her inventiveness failed her. Then he strode out to the start of the jetty, and she held back a gasp of admiration. He was wearing white jeans and a pale blue tee-shirt. His hair was ruffled by the wind, and he was smiling as though they had always been the best of friends. 'Long John Silver reporting for duty, sir,' he called.

He neared her, walking with confident strides along the jetty till he reached the *Speedwell*. Amy was slightly relieved that after a brief nod at her, he gave the little craft his full attention. She tried not to admire his figure as he looked *Speedwell* over, then said, 'Permission to come aboard?'

The wind was freshening, and *Speedwell* tugged at her moorings. Amy could see the enthusiasm in Chris's face. 'You take her,' she said, shifting to the bows and leaving him to take the tiller, and let out the sheet so that the sail filled and billowed, eager to be off. Amy loosened the painter, and they took off with an exhilarating burst of speed into the middle of Daweswater. There was no other traffic on the lake, apart from a solitary fisherman, sitting like a statue, his rod and line trailing in the sunlit water, in his small rowing-boat.

Chris seemed to forget Amy, as he handled the boat as though he had always sailed her. 'She's not a bad little craft!' he shouted. His face was alive with delight as he caught the wind, slowly slackened the sheet, and changed course for the end of the lake. Amy sensed what he was doing, and got her head out of the way without needing to be told the boom was coming over. She ceased to feel either selfconscious or apprehensive, but just settled down to enjoy the physical pleasure that a good boat and a lively wind can bring.

They crossed and recrossed the lake before Chris began to worry about getting home. 'I'd love to see how she goes on a bigger stretch of water,' he said.

'We took her to Derwentwater once,' Amy told him.

'We?'

'Larry Ford came with me. It was good, except the wind wasn't much that day.'

'I'll let you know next time I'm coming, and you get that trailer hitched up for me. Ready about!' They swerved, moving in rhythm with their boat, and set course for the jetty. Chris brought *Speedwell* alongside as though he had been doing it all his life, with scarcely a bump as Amy jumped out and moored. Without thinking, she held out her hand to Chris, and he took it with his usual firm grip as he leapt lightly to the jetty beside her. He kept her hand in his, as they turned to walk up to the Manor.

'Where do you usually sail?' She tried to speak normally, though her mouth had dried again.

'Greek Islands. I don't have a boat, but you can hire them out there. I try to go every summer.'

'Is that why you never came to see your father?'

Chris let go of her hand. Period of truce over, then. 'You do see me as some sort of villain, don't you, Amy? I came from school until Mum died. I didn't get to know Veronica too well. I didn't—well, it's a long story, but I made my own friends at school and university, and as she didn't need me and I didn't need her—well, Four Winds didn't really feel like home any more.'

That explained a lot. Why he was so different from Dr Mac, why he had turned into a city-dweller. The blue-haired Veronica—yes, she wasn't really the homely type, the self-effacing helpmeet that someone as devoted as Dr Mac needed. Chris had had to become self-sufficient; he had had no alternative.

'It does seem strange that you never even visited Greyrigg until your father died,' Amy pursued.

'It wasn't deliberate, just that my practice grew so rapidly. I didn't spend much time with Dad—and when I came, it was only to Four Winds. I always felt like a visitor in Cumbria. And when I came, the weather was always foul. I've never known it so lovely as the last couple of days.' They had come to the kissing gate, and Chris stood back to let her go first. Their eyes met as she closed the gate so that he could get through his side. He smiled at her, but maybe not with his eyes. 'I spent my holidays with Dad sitting by log fires drinking whisky.'

Chris came into the Manor to say goodbye to everyone. Amy stood back as he shook hands with the residents, and more warmly with Sharla and Quintin. The two of them walked with him to the gate, while Amy stood at the portico, watching, wondering if he would spare her a last glance. The Major had limped up to stand beside her, and Graham and Edna Bell joined them to give the young man a last wave. Amy could tell that most of them were charmed by young Dr Mac.

Aggie Brown was less restrained. She knocked vigorously on a window, and Chris turned, and his face brightened with a laugh as he waved just as vigorously back. 'I won't forget you, Aggie. I won't forget any of you,' he called cheerfully.

'Stay to lunch,' came Aggie's shrill voice.

'Can't—I'm late already.'

Gwyn Jones came out then, with a silver foil packet in her hand. 'You'd better take a sandwich,' she told him. Amy looked around. The entire population of Greyrigg seemed set on showing Chris their affection.

Chris turned and made it to the portico in a few long strides. Amy quite agreed with Aggie's sigh of admiration, 'Ee, I wish I were fifty years younger!' Amy couldn't hide her sudden giggle as Chris came up to them and took the packet with polite thanks.

Quintin and Sharla were standing near the gate, waiting for Chris to return and say his goodbyes. But Chris, tall and striking in his jeans, his muscles shown off by the short-sleeved tee-shirt, paused in front of Amy. His eyes were definitely hostile now, as though his patience was exhausted. But he took care not to let the others see his expression, as he said, 'Well, we didn't actually get anywhere, did we? And there's no time now. But I'll make you a fair offer. Be honest, and do a survey of your own on Greyrigg—as I've asked Quint to do. Then let me see it. Try to be objective, and forget all that sentimental twaddle you were going on about last night.'

'You make yourself quite clear,' she said coldly.

'Amy, I'm meeting you more than halfway. Now I'm far too busy to want to be troubled by my new responsibilities, so I'm leaving you to play fair with me. And who knows, if you get your report to me before Quint does, I might even not need his.

It could almost be a stranger, compared with the shining-eyed man she had sailed with that morning. Involuntarily she looked down at his brown slim fingers, that had tried to hold hers this morning, tried to get his own way by being nice. But she had to admit that this offer seemed fair. She knew she could do it, and better than Quintin too. 'I'll do it,' she promised.

'Good.'

'And I'll do it by logic, not sentimental twaddle.'

'The ball's in your court,' Chris told her.

He was already down at the bottom of the drive before she realised he hadn't actually said goodbye to her. He had shaken hands with every single person but Amy Taggart.

Threats, appeasement, kisses—he had certainly tried them all on Amy. But he was going now, and with any luck wouldn't be back. She still had the awful Quintin, but at least she had the chance of proving him redundant. She saw the others lifting their hands in a final salute, and lifted hers too, in a salute of defiance. Chris MacFarlane would learn that a country girl was as good as a city slicker any day! And she clenched her fist as he was lost to view behind the tall yew hedge and the carved stone gatepost.

CHAPTER THREE

'WELL NOW, Amy, that's over.' Gwyn Jones' Welsh lilt pierced Amy's thoughts. 'Maybe you could give me a hand with the lunch? How many would like to eat in the garden?'

Amy pulled herself down to earth. 'I'll ask. Have you the tablecloths?' They had left garden tables out now for the past month, as the heatwave had persisted through June and July. She wiped the tables and shook out clean white cloths, while Hannah and Gerry came round with cutlery.

'He's a hard act to follow.' Gerry was only trying to be chatty, but Amy had to bite her tongue to stop herself from snapping at him. 'Bit of a tornado, the way he swept in and zoomed out again. And how about that car! Every man's dream car, isn't it?'

Amy was prim. 'It's only money, Gerry. It may be a smart car, but give me Dr. Ford's little Land Rover any time. Dependable, fast, made for this place; and no show-off. That's what I like.'

'I think we should give the chap a chance to show us what he can do. He's made all the right noises.' Gerry polished the forks before setting them neatly on the cloth Amy had just laid. 'I must say it looks as though —well, that you've taken a dislike to him without knowing him properly.'

She straightened her back and smiled up at the big but not very bright Gerry. 'Go and get the salt and pepper from Gwyn, and stop dreaming of other men's cars!'

Just then a van came hurtling up the drive, pipping its horn. Gerry went to meet it. 'It's from Allie's Off-Licence.' He bent to speak to the driver, who jumped out and went round to open the doors. 'We didn't order any drinks, Allie. We didn't, did we, Amy?'

'I certainly didn't.' Amy walked down the lawn. 'Hello, Allie. What have you got there?'

Allie was small and bald, and had a constant smile. 'Someone up there likes you, Amy Taggart. Here you are—to be delivered to the Manor at lunchtime.' He handed her a box with four bottles, green bottles with gold tops.

'Champagne?' she gasped.

'No less, my dear. All paid for too. Here, Gerry, take it off me.'

A card dropped from the top as Gerry let the box tilt, and Amy bent for it, almost knowing who had sent it. The message was simple: 'With my warmest good wishes to all at Greyrigg. Dr Mac the Second.'

There was a cheer from the assembled guests as Amy read it. She felt herself burning with annoyance, that he could steal in and make a good impression even when not there in person. Still, trying to suppress her—did she admit it was prejudice?—she allowed Gerry and Hannah to open two bottles and give everyone a little taste. 'No, Aggie. It will play havoc with your blood sugar. Did you take your tablet?'

The Major stood up, wobbling a little as the painful hip took the strain. 'May I propose a toast to Dr Mac? He's a good fellow.'

There was an assenting chorus, 'To Dr Mac the Second.' And Amy drank with them, missing old Dr Mac, but perhaps glad that the guests were not left despondent by his death. That Christopher was a calculating devil! He must be chuckling to himself as he sped down the M6, imagining this little scene. Even when he wasn't here, she felt he had the edge over her. He knew he was going to win her over. And she knew equally well that he was not.

Lunch was prolonged and quite merry, thanks to the champagne. Amy found herself sitting on the stone steps up to the terrace, basking in the warm sun, and thinking that Greyrigg in summer was the next best thing to paradise. 'Amy? You asleep?'

It was Sharla, looking cool and pretty in a navy and white cotton dress. In spite of her lovely looks, Sharla wasn't in the least aware of her beauty. She was modest, friendly and helpful. Amy smiled. 'Come and relax, Sharla. Where have you been?'

'With Quintin—he has been looking over the old barn. Amy, it would make the most wonderful physio wing. Is anyone else using it?'

Amy's hackles rose at the idea of Quintin taking over. Yet she had to admit that the old barn was very under-used, being only a storeroom for most of the time. 'Sharla, it may be the champagne, but the old barn is yours. Just keep me informed about what you intend to do. And what about equipment? We can't really afford much new at present.'

'I've been checking all we've got. I suppose walking aids are available when they are needed?'

Amy explained, 'We can always get zimmers when we need them. We have a special fund. Our guests are mostly comfortably off, and we don't trouble the Health Service unless we can't find the gadgets privately.'

'Have we any Urias splints?'

'I'm sure we have. But they haven't been needed. I suppose we ought to check, to make sure they still inflate properly.'

'I'll do it, Amy. That's what Chris employed me for.'

Amy looked up at the elegant figure. 'Sharla, I really am glad you came. But I wonder why Chris employed you before checking on what facilities we had already?'

The Indian woman looked down suddenly, revealing her dark silky eyelashes. Her hands twined together. Amy felt like an intruder on some private feelings, and wished she had not been so direct. But Sharla looked up quickly. 'Have we a Flowtron machine?' she asked.

'No. Ought we to have? We have no stroke patients.'

Sharla nodded, her glossy hair swinging round her olive face. 'If I do my job properly, then we ought to be prepared for strokes. I've had some remarkable recoveries in St Martin's. I've got some of my notes, if you'd like to see them some time. I've worked with geriatrics all my working life—sorry, Amy, I know you don't like the word.'

At that moment there was the sound of a car engine in the lazy afternoon, and both girls looked up, to see Larry Ford's Land Rover bumping up the drive. He climbed out, with his stethoscope and little black bag clinging to his person. He was a tall boyish figure, his straw-coloured fringe hiding bright intelligent eyes. Amy called a greeting, and he ran up the stone steps to join them. 'Hello, ladies. Is it convenient for me to check your guests? I haven't quite fitted the Manor into my routine, but as I'm free this afternoon, I thought I'd pop in.'

Amy explained to Sharla, 'It sounds cold-blooded, but if anyone does die, it makes the certification much easier if they've all been seen within a fortnight. And of course, they do all need prescriptions. And they look forward to seeing any visitors, especially Larry.'

'Don't flatter, Amy. I have to live up to Dr Mac, remember? And that's hard.'

It was Sharla who said, 'No, Larry. You are a beloved visitor here.' And the young doctor looked away quickly, his cheeks unmistakably pink under the straw-coloured hair.

'Now, where shall I start?' he asked.

Amy led him to the Major, who was just nodding off. 'Major Hendon, just have a word with Dr Ford before you take your nap. You do need more of your arthritis tablets, don't you?'

The consultations went on, and Hannah was efficient to take the patients to their rooms for their afternoon rest. 'I rather like garden consultation,' smiled Larry, as a wood-pigeon cooed lovingly in the trees above him. Then his face changed. He was taking the pulse of Mrs Bell, who was usually called the Professor by the other residents, because she and her husband Graham had both been Oxford dons. 'This is irregular. Do you mind if we go to your room for a better examination?' And as Hannah obliged, Larry said to Amy, 'Has she complained of any palpitations?'

Edna Bell was on the way in, but she turned and said in her precise way, 'I didn't feel as well as usual, Dr Ford, but I associated it with upset over the funeral. The loss of our dear friend was quite a shock.'

Larry followed her in. 'I understand. Like losing a relative, I'm sure. It was for our practice too.'

On examination Amy stayed with them. She could see from Larry's face that there was a problem. Then she saw him examine the ankles for oedema. She ought to have noticed that herself: the ankles were swollen—signs of left ventricular failure. But it would respond to treatment, surely.

Larry wrote out a prescription. 'If these don't help, Amy, let me know at once, and I'll get Phil Harris to come out and do an ECG. She ought to have mentioned this to you.'

'I should have noticed. I suppose my mind was all on the funeral.' And on Chris MacFarlane, Amy could have added, and felt ashamed of her obsession with such a worthless successor to Dr Mac. 'I'll take more care in future,' she told him.

As they left Edna in her husband's care, Larry said, 'Her BP's high, Amy. I'll order some Centyl K for a week or two. But I'll get Carrington to do a domiciliary visit the moment he gets back from his holidays.'

'I'll drive her into Kendal if you like,' Amy offered.

'No, I'm sure it'll wait—she leads such a quiet life. I can't see any immediate danger. Just keep an eye on her.'

They went back into the sleepy garden, where the bees buzzed in the creeper and the roses, and the wood-pigeons' monotonous song lulled them into calm. Larry wrote out the last of the prescriptions, and put a rubber band round the sheaf. 'I'll pop these in to the chemist for you. They'll deliver in the morning.'

Just then Quintin Forbes came round the corner, dressed in a yellow shirt with no sleeves, grey slacks, and with a gold chain around his right wrist. Amy tried to be nice. 'You should be resting,' she told him. 'It's too hot to work.'

'What's the chinless wonder been up to?' Larry hissed in her ear.

Amy gave him a mock frown. 'Come and join us, Quintin.' And as he obeyed, his face revealing nothing, she said, 'Getting to know the place, are you?'

'Architecturally, Greyrigg is a jewel.' Quintin lolled on a seat, and accepted fresh lemonade from Mary Ledbetter. 'But my dear, so run down! The very fabric will be expensive to repair.'

'We can afford it,' Amy said stoutly. 'You weren't thinking of knocking anything down, were you? Our guests aren't poor. We can raise money for repairs. It's just that nobody thought of doing it.'

Quintin wobbled his head indecisively. 'It really depends on Chris. I'm just an adviser. But I do know he wants to do up the barn.'

'I've no quarrel with that, it will make a good physio room, but you have to remember it isn't heated at present. There's an emergency generator in the yard, but the electrics will need skilled advice.'

'Don't worry your pretty head about the details.' Quintin took a delicate sip from his glass, little finger akimbo. 'I've done more restorations than you might think. And you don't have to pay for my services—Chris is footing the bill.'

Amy went in as soon as Larry had taken his leave. The sunlight was dappling the hall floor with splashes of light that brought out the richness of the wood, How could anyone take away the character of Greyrigg? It was so gracious, so comfortable, so aristocratic. From what Quintin said, he wanted it turned into a holiday camp. She began her paperwork, entering the guests' visit from the doctor, and those who had prescriptions. But her heart felt heavy, and it took an effort to work.

She began to think about what Chris had said. If she prepared her own report he would look at it. Hannah

Briggs stopped at the office. 'Like a cuppa, Amy? Everyone's resting, so I thought I'd put my feet up.'

'Yes, thank you.' Amy put down her pen. 'Hannah, tell me—what do you think needs doing to the Manor?'

Hannah smiled. 'You thought of this because of that silly-looking fellow going round prodding things? When you come to think of it, we haven't been painted for a long time, inside or out. Some of the windowsills are crumbling. But apart from that, it's fine to work in.'

'Thanks.' Amy pulled out a clean sheet of paper and clipped it on a clipboard. Instead of trailing round the house 'prodding' as Quintin was doing, she had a better idea. She would get a personal report from every resident in the Manor. That would show Chris MacFarlane what the people who lived there really wanted. She began to get excited. It was a brilliant idea. But she must do it before Quintin finished his plan for Fantasy Island. Leaving the tea that Hannah had brought, she went in search of Gwyn Jones. 'Gwynny, tell me exactly what kind of a kitchen you'd like if you could re-design this place just as you wanted it?'

She had to be careful not to interview anyone when Quintin was around, in case he got suspicious, or tried to copy her ideas. Sharla Chowdray she took into her confidence, although she was a friend of Quintin. 'I think I know you well enough to trust you, Sharla,' she told her.

'I think I know you well enough to say how happy I have been here—happier than at any time in my life.' The dark eyes were sincere, wide and slightly tearful.

Amy said, 'At first I thought you looked like any successful London career woman. But now I can say I've noticed you looking most terribly sad—when you think no one's looking.' Sharla looked down, apparently reluctant to say more. Amy said, 'I didn't mean to say anything, but I saw the light band of skin on your third finger—where a ring must have been until quite recently.'

Sharla met her gaze for a second, then she looked

away, saying briefly, 'A wedding ring. Amy, do you have enough spare cash for a trans-cutaneous nerve stimulator? It would help the Major quite a lot. And one or two of the others. It's much better than a heat lamp, but it has to be used regularly.'

Amy reached for her clipboard. 'Right, you have all the cash you need! Assuming that the heating problem is overcome in the old barn, give me a list of all you really want.'

'Really? Oh, I see—this is to present to Chris. Well, I'll try to be realistic. But you have a variety of conditions here, and are likely to have others. Are you ready? Start with plenty of floor mats—really comfortable ones. Then of course the very latest heat lamps. Interferential machine. Beds, of course, for heat treatments and for postural drainage . . .'

'Hang on, I don't do shorthand!' Amy scribbled away as fast as she could. 'Can we get a few brochures to give us the cost of all these?'

'I'll see to it right away.' Sharla was smiling. 'I say, with that sort of department, I guarantee you eighteen healthy patients, you know. Even Frank Bates——'

Amy wasn't sure. 'Frank isn't all there, Sharla. Wouldn't it confuse him more to be pushed around?'

'Not in my experience. Let me give it a try, Amy. And I'll tell you what I'd like very much—a record player or cassette. I've found that ballroom dancing not only helps with balance and exercise—it is fun, too. Can I try that?'

'I'm not sure about that. Won't they feel as though they're being bullied? Dr Mac used to say leave them alone, they need their rest after a lifetime's work.'

'But I won't force anyone.' Sharla was pleading now. 'Amy, people age quicker if they are idle—I've seen it. Please let me assess each one individually, and work out a programme that would help them personally.'

Amy put her pen down and tried to make sense of her scribbles. 'I won't argue now. But let me know about progress, in case there's a medical reason why some of them shouldn't take too much exercise.'

'Will do.' Sharla got up to go, tossing back her dark mane of hair. 'And one of these days I'll explain about Ray.' She turned and went away very quickly, before any more questions could be put. Amy completed her report in neater longhand, wondering what Sharla's secret could be. Then she heard someone coming, and slid the notes under a pile of letters. It had to be kept secret from Quintin.

Amy found herself watching Quintin like a spy. Everything he looked at, she tried to match with ideas of her own. He made such detailed drawings and notes, and the more he sat hunched over his file, the more she wanted to see, but dared not ask.

Eventually she decided she would have to sneak into his room and take a look. She was nervous about such a procedure, having lived a blameless life up to now, open and honest and straightforward. But when she had tried that with Quintin—asking him straight out if she could see some of his drawings—he gave a loose-lipped grin and said slyly, 'Now, now, Amy! This is my job, not yours. I'm to report direct to Chris.'

Something in Amy prodded her to try the devious way. 'Surveying is thirsty work, Quintin. Why don't I take you along to the Pheasant? You do like real ale, don't you?'

'You mean there's a pub close by? Why didn't you tell me? I've been buying tinned lager.'

'I know, I've seen it in Gwyn's fridge. Come on, I'll treat you to Tom Bright's special brew. That'll put hairs on your chest!' She had tried Tom's special, and knew that its innocent taste concealed quite a punch. Quintin would surely sleep well after a glass or two—and she could feel safe about wandering in to take a peep at his papers. 'What a crook you're making me into, Chris MacFarlane!' She put away her work, and met Quintin at the front door.

'The Pheasant is an excellent example of the original unspoiled Lakeland pub,' Amy began, preparing Quintin for a treat, and trying to speak in a way to appeal to his love of the quaint, as well as his thirst. 'Oak beams, stuffed fish, valuable old prints and genuine horse brasses and shepherds' crooks.'

'I can't wait. Is it far? We could take the car.'

'Only a step. And you might not be able to steer straight on the way back.' Quintin took it as a joke, but Amy knew better.

They strolled in the warm evening, the air heavy with the scent of honeysuckle, gay with dog daisies, butter-cups and Queen Anne's Lace. The evening lay on the lake like a gossamer mantle. The contented quacking of a family of ducks echoed across the still water. Amy felt her criminal intent was out of tune with the perfection of nature—yet she was doing it in a good cause, so it had to be excusable. She smiled at Quintin, and pointed out the roof of the pub, nestling in a hollow round the next bend in the road.

She felt a sudden pang of sadness as she walked in and smelt the familiar wood and old beer smell. The last time she had been here was with Dr Mac. But she hid her emotion, knowing that Quintin wouldn't under-stand. She led the way to the bar. 'Evening, Tom,' she smiled.

'Evenin', Amy. Keepin' all right?' Tom Bright was gruff and jolly and very fat. 'Who've you brought along, then?'

'This is Quintin, he's doing some work at the Manor.' Amy began to lay it on thick, knowing that Tom would understand but Quintin wouldn't. 'He's from London, Tom, and he's very clever!'

'Oh aye?' Tom grinned at Quintin, who stepped forward, to the great fascination of the locals. He was wearing loose trousers, fashionable in London but merely baggy here. And his Fair Isle sweater over pink silk shirt, with loosely knotted cravat, looked like fancy dress. Amy suggested they sit in an alcove to prevent embarrassment, but no such thing! Quintin enjoyed the attention. 'They probably don't have many good men's fashion shops round here,' he whispered, basking in the open glances, attributing them to envy of his fine plumage.

Amy hid her smile in a glass of beer. 'Cheers, Quintin.'

'Cheers, darling.' He drank off his pint in one swig. Amy shuddered at the effect it would have as soon as he started to walk home, but he snapped his fingers for another, with no apparent damage yet.

'Tell me about Chris,' she invited. 'Where did you meet him, Quintin?'

Quintin set his glass down and snapped his fingers again for some peanuts. 'We were at Westminster together. We weren't too friendly in the first forms, I must say. He was terrific at games, and I was more the academic type, you know. But when he took a fancy to my sister Francesca, we started seeing a lot of each other. He used to come with our family on holidays to Greece—we have a villa on Kos. Then we made up a foursome with Fran's chum Sonia, and did the sailing bit with a flotilla. It terrified me at first, darling, honestly, even in the Aegean, which is warm as toast and lovely and calm most of the time. Ever been to Greece, Amy love?'

He was getting affectionate. Good—he might be more frank about his work. 'Never. Tell me about it.' She didn't want to know, but she did want his trust.

Quintin proceeded to list the exotic holidays he and Chris had spent with 'the girls'. From the way he spoke, Francesca was still very much a part of Chris's life. Amy pretended to be interested, but her opinion of Chris didn't change; it was still low. She began to yawn after a while, but she reminded herself she was in a war situation here, a war she had to win. So she sat on the stool while Quintin held forth about his favourite subject —Quintin.

After his third beer his speech began to slur. Amy bore it all, sticking to tomato juice so that she didn't miss any gems of information he might drop. But it became more and more boring, as Quintin related all the famous houses he had been commissioned to restore and redecorate.

It must have been nearing midnight when they finally staggered home, Tom being notoriously lenient about last orders. The stars were bright, and the bats active in the elm trees. Quintin was in a very happy state of mind, and he clung to Amy's shoulders as they walked, explaining that the road was too winding for him to navigate. She permitted the familiarity, reminding herself that this would cement their relationship, which should pay handsome dividends as soon as she got into his room.

Once at Greyrigg, Quintin released Amy's shoulders and grabbed her hand, insisting on dragging her all round the outside, pointing out the features he had noticed. This was more like it! Amy listened carefully, while exhorting Quintin in a stage whisper not to wake the residents. After they had been all round, she looked back at the dear old stone walls, with a silent promise that no one should be allowed to change even a leaf of ivy if she had power to stop it.

The owl hooted near the portico, and Quintin jumped a foot into the air. Amy hid a giggle at his sudden fright, and explained that it was only a bird, not a banshee. 'Then why doesn't it sound like one?' he complained rather truculently. Then he threw an arm around her again. 'Put me to bed, Amy.'

She had no choice but to guide him up the staircase to the rooms that had so recently belonged to Dr Mac. Quintin made several stabs at the keyhole with his key. Finally Amy took it from him and opened the door. 'Good night,' she said firmly. 'Sleep well.'

'Don't go yet, Amy.' His voice was loud, and she pushed him inside before he woke anyone. Once inside, he grabbed her very tightly round the waist. 'Now I've got you, my pretty lady! I know a thing or two about women. You won't struggle any more, will you, Amy?'

She swallowed, hating the idea of this oaf in Dr Mac's room, and of the way she had been fooled by his pretence at the keyhole. 'I can see it's no use,' she shrugged. Her only hope was to regain his confidence. She stood completely still as he began to pull off his pullover. His shirt was out, and his cravat under one ear.

'I need a drink.' He crossed the room to the old bureau, which Dr Mac had kept full of notes and letters. In it now was a bottle of brandy and one of vodka. Amy's nose wrinkled in disgust. What would her friendly ghosts think of this interloper? She began to wish she had never thought of trying this form of industrial espionage.

Quintin came towards her again, two balloon glasses of brandy carefully held in both hands. She could easily run away now, but it would spoil the entire plan. 'I can't take brandy, Quintin. It makes me ill.'

'Just a little sip, love. Just a little sip.' His voice was very slurred now, and he slopped the drink as he tried to put one glass down. He reached out with one arm to grab her again, and she shrank from his grappling hand and his heavy breath.

Suddenly she heard footsteps. 'Shh!' She stood up and moved as far from him as she could. 'Someone's there!'

Quintin peered at the door. The footsteps had stopped. They both seemed to hold their breath—and then the doorknob turned, and the little figure of Aggie Brown entered. She wore a cotton nightdress with a collar and tucks down the front, and she looked like some naughty Victorian schoolgirl, with her wide blue eyes, her bare feet and hair in two bunches. She looked innocently at Amy. 'I dreamed that Dr Mac was here,' she told her. It was an unlikely explanation, but Amy hadn't the heart to scold her. She had arrived so very fortunately just in time.

'I'd better help you to bed, Aggie dear.' Amy put her arm round the thin shoulders and led her away, rejoicing in her escape. When she went back upstairs Quintin's door was still open, but loud snores could be heard from the landing. The light was still on. She took off her shoes and crept into the room, making for the desk where she had seen him working. It was locked.

Deflated, she was just about to turn away when she saw a file of papers on the chair, pushed under the desk. She drew it out. Yes—here were some of the drawings, with pencilled recommendations. Amy leafed through them as fast as she could, trying to memorise the details, then she replaced the file where she had found it, and went back to her room. It was very late. She had worked hard for that small success, but before she went to sleep she noted down as much of Quintin's work as she could remember.

Quintin, fortunately, had no knowledge of the last moments in his room. All he remembered was having a few drinks with Amy. Satisfied, she maintained a good relationship with him, without making the mistake of being alone with him again. Yet she noticed that although they were more chatty together, he never allowed her to look over his shoulder when he was drawing or writing. 'Secrets, Amy love. Secrets,' he would coo. And she would pretend to be disappointed, though she had in fact learned enough of his plans to be able to work out arguments against them. It had been a famous victory. Amy was feeling more confident now. All that remained was to type up her notes and let Chris MacFarlane have them.

But when he called, she was not expecting it. She was in the garden, watching Arthur Taylor as he tended his three beehives behind the vegetable patch. His wife Ruth came out, and Amy thought she had come to talk to her husband, but she said breathlessly, 'It's the telephone for you, Amy. He sounded dead posh. And ordered me about, he did! Get her at once, please, he said, all bossy like.'

'I'll see about that.' Amy marched back along the crazy paving, annoyed that a member of her staff should be spoken to so rudely. 'Hello? This is Sister Taggart.' She waited, ready to snap back the moment the caller identified himself.

'Hello, Amy Taggart.'

She felt as though all the breath had gone out of her.

Instead of the rebuke she had planned, she heard herself saying weakly again, 'Hello.'

'You recognise me, then? Chris here.'

'I should have known.' She had recovered from the shock, pulled her defences together. 'No one else would have been rude to Ruth.'

'I wasn't rude—I'm just in a hurry, that's all. When she said you were down the garden, I knew you had quite a way to get here.' Chris paused. When she didn't reply he said, 'Sorry.'

'Why are you ringing in the middle of the day?' Amy asked. 'Is it urgent?'

'My next patient is late. I thought I'd check with you to see if you're ready to meet me over the alterations business.'

'As a matter of fact, I am almost ready.'

His voice changed, as he said, 'You know, when I hear you, I can't help thinking of the lake and the hedgerows and the fresh air. You'd be appalled at the traffic fumes I'm getting through this window!'

Impatiently she said, 'Do you want to speak to Quintin about his report?'

'Certainly not. Done any sailing lately?'

'A bit.' Amy decided to hit home a little. 'I daren't leave the Manor for long in case Quintin does something dreadful behind my back.'

There was a splutter that could have been a laugh. 'Amy, you're nice!'

'Pity I can't say the same about Quintin,' she retorted. 'You ought to have warned me he was the amorous type.'

His voice hardened. 'He hasn't been—Amy, I'm sorry. You haven't been . . .'

'Don't worry,' she assured him. 'I coped.'

In the background she could hear a woman's voice. Chris said, 'Excuse me a second——' and faintly she heard scraps of conversation. 'No, angel, not tonight . . . tickets? . . . oh, I see, white tie . . . okay, pencil that in, and phone Francesca . . . no, BMA meeting . . .

Tavistock Square . . . not more than a thousand . . .'
And then he came back to the phone. 'I'm sorry, Amy,
but my patient's arrived. Try to get down to see me,
would you? I need to be kept in the picture. 'Bye, Amy
Taggart.'

   She put the phone down. What a telling glimpse into
his life! It sounded dreadful—all fumes and fuss and
artificiality. She looked out of the window at the lake
glistening between the trees and felt better. Let Chris
stay in his own world. It was no place for Amy Taggart.

CHAPTER FOUR

As AMY went across the long meadow each morning for the newspapers, she noticed that her thoughts, however wrapped up in the affairs of Greyrigg, always turned to the day of the funeral—the day she had first met Chris MacFarlane. His tall lean frame, his sharp blue eyes, and his crisp challenging manner were images that recurred in her mind whenever she was alone.

But now they were intertwined with visions of the beautiful Francesca. Amy had stopped the youthful frisking she used to do with Nell, and her way over the meadow was thoughtful and solemn. She couldn't forget Chris—how could she, when she was locked in combat with him? But on the other hand, his life was just so incredibly different from her own. He was the high flier, the tycoon, whose glamorous life she had caught a glimpse of on the phone. Surely there was no point in going on with this fight? They were diametrically opposed in attitude. How could they ever agree over Greyrigg Manor? And how could Amy, the underdog, ever hope to win?

Her own report was almost ready, carefully and painstakingly typed out, with many a reference to the comfort of the residents, the convenience for the staff. Mr Gately had more to worry about now than affairs at Greyrigg. 'Mornin', Amy love. How's the beck up yon fell near you?'

'Still running, Mr Gately. But getting very small.'

'We'll have standpipes before long, I'll be bound. It's same as it were seven year ago.' He looked worried. 'Have you seen the river? Nobbut a trickle.'

'I hear they're rationing in Borrowdale,' said Amy. 'That's a laugh—the wettest valley in the country!'

'If I were you, I'd collect some of that beck water. With your old folk, you have need of it more'n us fit ones.'

'I'll see to that, Mr Gately. Thanks.'

Amy reached the Manor, and noticed someone in the garden. So soon? Breakfast wasn't served yet. She dumped the papers on the sideboard and went round to check. 'Oh, it's you, Quintin.'

'Morning, love. Want to see?' He held out the pad he was sketching on.

She had got used to his affected voice by now. But it was a shock to be offered a sight of his work. He held out the drawing in front of her. It was a pencil sketch of the Manor, and it was beautiful. 'What do you think?'

'Quintin, you're a real artist!' She gazed at the work, amazed at the way he had built the sunshine into a black and white drawing. 'Just look at the roses by the portico! You can almost smell them.'

He seemed delighted with her approval. 'All part of the job, of course. I'll be pencilling in some recommendations.'

'Oh, don't spoil it. Let me have it, please? I'll pay the proper price. I'd like to frame it.'

'And there was I thinking you'd bite my head off for suggesting alterations!'

Amy smiled. 'As you yourself said, it's Chris who makes the final decision. I'm meeting him shortly for a chat about our future.'

'Where?' Quintin looked worried. 'When? You aren't going all the way to London, are you? He's far too busy to have time for you there.'

Amy was wise enough not to press the point. Quintin was rattled—that meant he wasn't at all sure his own proposals would be acceptable either. That gave her a lot of confidence. She changed the subject, noticing the relaxation in his pale eyes. 'Come on now, sell me the picture? Twenty pounds?'

'You want to give me that much bread for a ten-minute sketch?'

'I like it,' Amy told him.

'You can have it for ten.'

'Quintin, you're a real gentleman.' She held out her

hand, and he joined in her smile. 'That's what I call a bargain.'

Their tranquil conversation was interrupted by a shrill shout from the house. Hannah came out, running as fast as Amy had ever seen her. 'Amy, Amy, I can't get hold of Dr Ford. It's Edna—it's a stroke. She's unconscious!'

'Call the ambulance, then.' Amy was on her feet, running back with her. 'No, I'll take her, it's quicker. Will you ring and alert AED? Say I'll be there in half an hour.' She dashed indoors, where half of the guests were down in the dining room finishing their breakfasts.

It was Aggie Brown who called Amy from the first floor. 'She's still in her room. It was Graham who called Hannah. Hurry, Amy love, he's all upset.'

The poor lady was just conscious, but very bewildered by being unable to move her left arm and leg. Her face was white, her lips blue, and her eyes rolled in her head as Graham knelt with his rheumaticky limbs and put his arm under her head. 'I'm here, Edna. I'm here, dear.' Amy's heart was touched by the anguish in his eyes. She knelt and examined Edna. There wasn't much question of the diagnosis—it was a fairly severe stroke. But at least her eyes were focusing now, and she knew where she was, and even what day it was.

'Ask Arthur and Dan to bring the stretcher.' Amy turned to Graham. 'You musn't worry, Graham—she'll get better. But I'll be happier if she goes to hospital overnight—just for supervision, seeing that her heart condition hasn't been stabilised yet.'

The old man was noble in his grief. With head erect he said, 'Of course, Amy, I do understand,' in his clipped correct English. Then he broke down and cried.

It was Damaris Jarvis who took him to her motherly bosom. She was the one Chris had called the 'pretty one'. She had cared for Flo Walters for many years, ever since they were both farmers' wives, and Flo had developed muscular dystrophy. She was still very dominant, and cared for Flo like her own daughter. But there was room in her heart for Graham too. 'Now you'd be best coming down with us, Graham love,' she soothed. 'You can't do much for Edna just now—that's doctors' work. We'll let them get on with it, and wait till they bring her back to us.' And she took his hand like a child and led him out to sit with herself and Flo—three dignified little figures, trying to cope with the tragedies of life by quiet courage and human sympathy.

Amy had decided they needed the proper ambulance. With Edna's cardiac problems, she knew they might have an arrest, and she wanted her somewhere where the correct equipment was available. But she promised faithfully not to leave Edna, and sat by her side all the jolting journey to Kendal, holding her hand and stroking it in reassurance.

She was well acquainted with the physician at the hospital, Phil Harris, who often came out to see her residents when Larry and Dr Mac had needed a specialist opinion. 'Who have you brought me, Amy?' Phil asked her.

'It's Edna Bell, Phil. She——'

'Don't tell me! She was on my list for a domiciliary. I would have come to see her tomorrow.'

'She's saved you a journey. Left hemiparesis.' They were on the way to the ward now, Edna awake but comatose on a trolley. 'Larry did digitalise her, but she only started the tablets a few days ago.'

'Right.' They got Edna to bed. 'Hello, Edna. Feeling a bit brighter now? That's very good, my dear.' Phil looked across at Amy. 'Are you waiting?'

'I'll pop back and have a word when you've finished the neuro examination.'

Phil did a thorough examination. After he had gone Amy crept back to the bedside. 'I've promised not to stay too long, but is there anything you want, Edna?' she asked.

The old lady reached out her right hand, and Amy took it. Edna said, 'I'm not afraid of dying, Amy. I've thought about it, and I can face it. But it's Graham. We've been together for sixty years, you know. He'll never survive without me.'

Amy sat down, and looked earnestly at her patient, looking strangely small and vulnerable, though she had once been a tall and striking woman. 'I know that, Edna. But you aren't dying just yet. I'll come and bring you back in a couple of days.'

'I suppose I have nothing to worry about really,' said Edna. 'I have complete faith in you and the other nurses. You'll look after him like the family he never had.'

'We promise,' Amy assured her.

'And he'll come after me . . .' Edna looked sharply at Amy. 'How did you know he wouldn't survive without me?'

Amy swallowed. It was hard to say. Her voice was hoarse as she said, 'My father died of cancer when I was young, and Mum only lasted six months after that.'

'Oh, my dear—so very young—no wonder you care for us all so lovingly. We must take your parents' place in your heart.'

'I'd never thought of it that way, Edna.' Amy patted the old hand. 'But you're right as usual. Now you must get some sleep while you're in here, then come back and Sharla will put some life in those misbehaving limbs of yours. She told me she has the instruments. All she needs is guts—yours!'

'I'll do my best.' Edna's smile was a trifle one-sided, but the light in her eyes showed that she was by no means beaten. 'See you tomorrow?'

'I'll bring Graham,' promised Amy.

It was only when she came out into the glare of late afternoon that she realised she had had no lunch. She wandered towards the bus station. Kendal was full of holidaymakers in shorts and shirts, with many sunburnt knees in evidence, and rucksacks of every shape and size. Amy went into a little café near the bus stop. Olive and Daniel would be on duty. They wouldn't forget Aggie's insulin, Lucy's eyebath or Frank Bates's incontinence bag, would they? It was all written down. She pulled herself together. She was going to London soon, so she'd better get used to Greyrigg functioning quite well without her.

'Thank goodness I found you, Amy!'

She looked up in surprise. It was Larry Ford. 'Hello. What are you doing here?'

'Come to take you back. Sharla called me and told me what happened. You went off in the ambulance. Why didn't you follow behind in your car?'

'Because Edna needed me to calm her down, that's why. I could easily have caught a bus to Keswick, and Billy Braithwaite would have given me a lift along lakeside. He's done it before.'

Larry sat down. 'I might as well share your pot of tea, seeing that I'm here.' He beckoned for a second cup and saucer. 'I searched inside the hospital first, then I decided you might have taken a taxi. But the bus station was nearer. I'm not used to all that walking, Amy. Tell me where to meet you next time.'

They exchanged a smile. 'Thanks anyway,' smiled Amy.

They drove back at a more leisurely pace, seeing on all sides evidence of the drought, the tinder-dry bracken and the empty becks. Larry was a good soul, but not a very vibrant conversationalist. His work was his life. After a silence he said hesitantly, 'How do you get on with Miss Chowdray?'

'Sharla? She's great. The guests took to her right away. She's planning on teaching them ballroom dancing.'

'I like her too. She seems a very dedicated person.' Did Amy perceive a hint of embarrassment at the admission? She gave a little jump in her seat. Wouldn't it be wonderful if Sharla could coax a spark of fire from this gentle but unawakened man? Yet there was a lot they didn't know about her. The wedding ring—and her mention of 'Ray'. It might be a little premature to try any matchmaking. All the same—Amy invited Larry back to Greyrigg for supper, and he accepted very readily indeed.

'But I have to admit I don't take to that other person there,' he told her.

Amy smiled at his description of Quintin as a 'person'. 'Oh, he livens things up a bit by his very oddness,' she shrugged.

Nell was sitting at the gate, keeping an eye on things. She jumped up when she saw Amy, and gambolled up the drive after the Land Rover. But all was not well. As Larry and Amy jumped out and went to the front door, Olive and Faith Hindle were standing on the steps, their faces worried and frowning. 'It's Frank Bates,' they told her. 'He's wandered off again.'

Poor Frank didn't really know where he was. But although he did tend to wander, it had never been far out of the gates before. Amy said briskly, 'He isn't that tough to get very far. Come on—two search parties. I take it Daniel and Arthur are out looking already?'

'Yes, they went up to the hazel woods.'

'Right. I'll go down to the village. Chuck me a whistle, Olive. First one to whistle has found him.'

Sharla was just coming out. 'Let me come too.'

Larry said, 'Me too. I'll try along the lakeside while you two go to the village.'

They had gone halfway across the long meadow when they heard a whistle. 'Thank goodness!' The three of them turned and ran back towards the Manor. Ruth and Arthur Taylor were standing at the gates. Arthur said, 'He's up in the woods, Amy, but his leg's hurt. Dan's with him. I've come for the stretcher.'

Larry took charge then. 'I'd better see him. Follow on, Arthur.'

'Right up the path—you can't miss him.'

Amy and Sharla tagged on too in case they were needed. They followed Larry up through the silver birch and hazel trees, lush and sweet-smelling in their full summer foliage. It was quiet up there, and Amy realised it was because the beck had ceased to flow. Only the occasional bleat of a sheep up on the fells echoed through the dappled wood.

Sharla puffed, 'I thought you said he wasn't very tough. This path is steep!' Larry Ford slowed his pace, and put out a hand to pull her up. 'They are just up there—I can see Nell.'

They staggered the last few steps, and Larry put out a hand to stop them. They crept up quietly to see what Larry and Daniel were looking at.

It was a sweet and touching sight. Little Frank Bates lay, his back against a silver birch, his white hair awry, looking up with his wild uncomprehending eyes at a small fallow deer. It showed no fear of him, merely curiosity, as he cooed in some strange language to it, a gentle smile on his usually sullen face. The three rescuers dared not move, dared not break that peculiar woodland magic. Even Nell, usually boisterous, sat back, ears pricked, looking intelligently at Amy.

The little creature sensed their nearness. It must have been scent. Eyes big and alert, it turned and at once was hidden among the trees. Frank's face slowly turned to its usual blankness, but it was a gentle blankness, perhaps showing that he carried the beauty of the little deer in his fading memory. Larry climbed up the last few steps and touched his arm. 'How are you, old chap? I think you'll need a hand down.' And as Frank turned his face towards him, Larry said, 'Teatime, old chum.'

The old man looked up, his hair a shaggy white halo round his head, then held out both arms, like a child. Larry and Daniel took an arm each, and they helped him on to the stretcher. 'Just a sprain.' Larry had swiftly felt both ankles. When they reached the Manor, he hoisted the old man up in his arms as he would a baby, to carry him up the steps and into the Manor.

Aggie Brown was waiting like any aggrieved wife might wait, hands on hips. 'Frank Bates, how dare you come home at this hour? Your tea will be spoilt!'

Larry laughed at her, and set the old man down on the settee in the hall, examining the ankle again. 'Now be kind to him, Aggie. I just want to take another look at this ankle.' Aggie took him at his word, and brought

Frank a mug of tea as the young doctor examined the weak joint. 'Ligament strain.' He went out to his Land Rover and came back with a crêpe bandage. 'This should do, if you make sure he doesn't do any ten-mile strolls for a week or two.'

'It was worth it, though.' Amy was still thinking of the dappled deer.

As she turned away, she almost collided with Graham Bell. 'Oh, my dear, I'm so sorry!' she apologised. 'I should have come to you at once. Edna is very comfortable and happy, and I'll take you to see her tomorrow.'

'That's good news.' Graham spoke as he had lived, as a lecturer, his face aristocratic with his long white hair wild and uncombed without his wife to check him. 'We've never spent very long apart.' Amy turned away suddenly, reminded of the plight of her own parents. Tea was brought in for everyone, but Amy had lost her appetite, and went up to her room to be by herself for a while.

It was later that night, when everyone had been helped to bed, and Greyrigg was hushed. Amy called it the time of the friendly ghosts, when she was sure it was possible to feel some link with the people who had lived in the Manor in earlier times, had enjoyed living there, and loved the place as much as she did. Dear, dear Dr Mac was with them now, she was sure. She knew it in her heart. She was sitting in companionable silence with Sharla and Hannah. Hannah was on nights and had brought her knitting. Sharla had just turned off the television. She said to Amy, 'Please stop me if you don't want to talk, but I thought you were very sad when you were talking to Graham Bell.'

'It was the way Edna and Graham are so devoted to each other,' Amy explained.

'They are close.'

Amy said, trying to explain, 'My parents, Sharla. I was born on a farm.'

'Near here?'

'Yes. Dad got lung cancer. Isn't it ridiculous, when he

never smoked in his life, and only drank sherry on special occasions. He was outdoors all his life.'

'Go on—if it helps.'

Amy looked across at Sharla, and knew she was speaking to someone who understood suffering. 'When he couldn't carry on the farm, we all went to stay with my uncle, at Bury, near Manchester. My uncle was a consultant at the general hospital there. Dad had the best treatment, of course. But he—died. And Mum—it was quite clear she didn't want to go on without him. They said it was kidney failure, but I know it was grief.'

Sharla said nothing at once, for which Amy was grateful. Then she said, 'Now there is only your uncle?'

'And his family. Auntie Jan and Cousin Madeleine, who's teaching English in Alsace Lorraine.'

'And you don't want to leave here?'

'Never. Edna was right. I've adopted Greyrigg as my family.'

Sharla said dreamily, 'I sometimes think of Kashmir, yet I am sure it does not belong to me. I am British. And since being here, I have never felt so peaceful.'

Amy had recovered her spirits. 'It's wonderful in summer. But are you sure you can take a Cumbrian winter, Sharla?'

The other girl laughed. 'Of course. I know what winter is—Chris took us skiing in Scotland. Now that is cold!'

Amy was suddenly struck dumb. She had thought Chris MacFarlane far from their thoughts, yet there he was. And she had to admit that he was very vivid in her own mind—skiing or sailing, enjoying life in his jet-set, fast-lane manner. Conversation flagged between the three friends. In the distance, soft piano notes filtered through the warm night.

Amy said as Hannah stirred, 'Leave her. It's Lucy. She told me once that the music in her heart becomes unbearable unless she can play it.'

It was Chopin again. Even at eighty, Lucy played superbly, with few mistakes, and a gentle touch. Such softness would not disturb the others. As the Nocturne came to an end, Amy went through to the dining room, where the old lady sat, straight-backed, her blind eyes brimming with tears. 'Is that you, Amy?' she asked.

'Yes, dear. That was beautiful.'

'I shouldn't be unhappy, Amy,' said the old lady. 'I sometimes miss my friends.'

'And aren't we your friends?'

'You are, I know. But Amy, youth does have something special. The people you know then—they stay with you for ever.' Lucy paused. 'Even the boy-friend you lose to someone more glamorous . . .'

Amy tried to prevent the self-pity. 'Those boy-friends aren't worth having—selfish and insensitive and boring!'

She succeeded in bringing a smile to Lucy's lips. 'I do know, dear. But I perhaps would have liked to have a selfish, insensitive boring young man of my own.'

Amy said candidly, as she led the old lady back to her room, 'You're right. Here I am—spinster of this parish at twenty-eight. I feel it, Lucy, though it isn't fashionable to say so.'

'Oh dear, what a great age!' Lucy was smiling. 'Good night, my dear. You're a sweet girl, and we all love you.'

Amy waited until Lucy was settled in bed, then she went back to the lounge, where Sharla was just getting ready to go up. 'I haven't seen Quintin today,' Sharla remarked.

'His car must be in the drive.'

'No.'

Amy said firmly, 'Quintin I don't worry about. He's probably gone into town looking for talent—there aren't enough women in Daweswater. He'll be back tomorrow, you'll see.'

'Probably.' Sharla wasn't too worried either. 'Good night, Amy.'

'Good night.' Amy began to realise how tired she was. She went upstairs, pausing for a word with Hannah. 'All right? Everyone in bed?'

'I had to give Frank a sedative,' Hannah told her. 'And the Major was in a lot of pain, so I gave him analgesics, but I bet he wakes up again. You don't know when they're going to send for him to have his hip done?'

'I'll give the hospital a ring, and get Larry to say it's urgent.'

'Good. Sleep well, Amy. You look all in.'

It had indeed been a busy day. Yet as she went slowly upstairs, Amy knew that Chris MacFarlane had been there at the back of her mind all day, disturbing her regular routine, reminding her that she was still vulnerable, still dependent on that superior, annoying but compelling personality. The confrontation was coming, and she knew she was terrified that her own admiration of him as a man would let her down when she had to be strong and firm, and show no weakness. Only time would tell. But Amy prayed for moral courage and strength that night.

There was no sign of Quintin next morning, and Amy grew increasingly irritated that he hadn't even bothered to let them know he was going away. But she was too busy to give him much attention. The Major was very stiff and uncomfortable. And Peggy Bickerstaffe, one of the very quiet ones who spent each day in the chair in which she was put and stared at the television all evening until they put her to bed, fell and bumped her head on the sideboard.

'She must have a skull X-ray today.' Amy was worried, although Peggy insisted she only had a headache.

Arthur Taylor offered to take her in to the hospital, but Amy wanted him to stay and help Daniel Feather. If the Major fell, or needed help, two men would be needed. 'I'm taking Graham to see Edna this afternoon,' she told him. 'I'll make them both comfy in the back of the estate, and make one journey to it. So long as I get there before X-Ray closes.'

It was a delightful ride, in spite of being en route to the hospital. The lake glittered and shone in the everlasting sun, the birds sang, and the trees, particularly the beeches, were clothed in finest fresh colours, full and lush and generous with shade. Amy chatted, to keep

Graham's spirits up. Peggy wasn't too talkative a person at the best of times.

There was a porter there, ready to help with the wheelchair. They delivered Peggy to X-Ray, with strict instructions not to move until they came back for her. The Sister there was an old friend of Amy's, so she knew they would do as she asked.

Edna Bell was lying on the pillows, her face composed but tense. 'Yes, I'm very comfortable,' she told Amy. 'But my leg is totally useless. I'll never walk again.'

'What does that matter? You're going to be all right.' Graham took her hand and patted it in delight at seeing her so alert and looking rested.

'Yes. Of course. It's still the same me, in spite of being defective in a few major parts.' She tried to lift her arm. There was some movement in the larger muscles, but Edna had no power in her fingers. 'You mean to tell me that just exercise can make that all right?'

Amy smiled and shook her head. 'Remember what I told you yesterday—exercise plus guts. You need both.'

She was glad that Sharla would be there when they took Edna home. She would know exactly how to manage her—and she would be delighted at the challenge. In spite of her personal unhappiness, which showed every so often, Sharla gave her patients nothing but cheerful encouragement and fun. But Phil Harris wouldn't allow Edna to go home with them. 'I want to keep an eye on the LV failure for another couple of days.' He smiled. 'I know it's a long way to visit, but it'll be worth it in the long term. She's basically a strong woman, and I want her to be on the correct medication.'

It was late when they got back, but Gwyn had kept their grilled plaice warm, and the three of them sat in the dining room, the lengthening shadows outside giving a rest from the constant heat of the sun. The crickets were chirping under the open window, and the scent of the roses wafted in.

Sharla came in to ask how Edna was, and smiled at Graham with confidence. 'She is a determined lady. I know I can help her, don't worry. I might even have her walking without a stick eventually, you'll see. It will be a joint effort—you and me and Edna.'

Amy liked the way she spoke—down to earth and without allowing for any self-pity. After they had all shared a pot of tea, Peggy wanted to go to her television chair. Graham took her, and Amy suddenly remembered Quintin.

'No sign yet,' said Sharla.

Amy said, 'He's either had an accident, or he's gone to see Chris. I've remembered the look in his eye when I told him I was going to London—he didn't like it.' She stood up. 'Before I phone the police and alert the mountain rescue, I'm going to phone Chris MacFarlane.'

'Of course! He's probably missing his old watering hole in Chelsea. It is very quiet here when you are used to town.'

'You don't mind it?'

'I love it—all peace and no hassle.' Sharla caught Amy's expression. 'Yes, I will tell you about my marriage—soon. The divorce is almost finalised, so I'll feel more secure when that's done.'

Amy's hand was shaking a bit as she looked up Chris's telephone number. He had insisted she write it down, but she had not intended ever to use it. She dialled slowly, making sure each digit was accurate. She waited, heart fluttering, as she heard the ringing at the other end. 'Hello? Dr MacFarlane?' His voice was deep, powerful, reassuring. That must be his bedside manner voice. 'It's Amy Taggart.'

'Yes, Amy.' The voice changed, and she was sure it sounded pleased. 'You're coming to London for our meeting?'

'I'm ringing to see if Quintin is there. He appears to have vanished without letting anyone know where he was going.'

'That was a bit cheeky. Yes, he came here with his plans—wanted some advice about costing.'

'Sharla says he was missing his old Chelsea

watering hole.'

'That too.'

'The selfish beast!' Amy exclaimed.

'I quite agree. He'll be back tomorrow. If I see him, I'll tell him he's in trouble from Matron. That'll scare him!'

Amy could hear the strains of a Haydn symphony in the background, and she wondered what kind of flat it was, and if he were alone. She said, irritated by his offhand tone, 'I've finished my report.'

'Hmm.' Chris sounded suddenly serious. 'I see. Well, I'd better take a look. When are you free?' He sounded like a consultant now, stern and businesslike.

She thought quickly. The sooner the better. Get it over, now that she had all her thoughts on paper. 'Day after tomorrow—Wednesday. I can get a cheaper ticket.'

'I'll meet the train. What time?'

'I don't know yet. Anyway, I can get a taxi. I wouldn't want to be a nuisance to a busy man like you.'

'Amy, I love you! See you on Wednesday afternoon, then.' And he put the phone down. His tone was light and amused. He hadn't really said what she thought he said? And if he had, he didn't mean it—he was being impertinent, treating her like an idiot. All the same, when she finally put the phone down after several seconds of listening to the tone, the words began to go round and round in her head. Naturally he was joking. But . . . Amy, I love you . . . Amy, I love you . . .

She bumped into Sharla on the stairs. 'I'm going to London on Wednesday,' she told her. 'Yes, Quintin was there. Me—deliberately leaving this place for a stuffy smelly unfriendly city!'

And then she turned in amazement, for Sharla's pretty face had crumpled. With both hands up to hide her face, she turned and ran back upstairs. Amy stood and watched, but didn't follow. When she tapped gently on the door before putting her light out, there was no answer.

CHAPTER FIVE

THE TRAIN'S regular speed made Amy sleepy. Rocking, gently rocking from side to side, she forgot to go over in her head all the major points she had to confront Chris MacFarlane with. She hadn't slept very well last night, going over and over the way she would confront him, the way she would not allow him to overrule her carefully reasoned manuscript. She stood up and lifted her brief-case down from the rack, even took out the file she had prepared. But they were still far from London, and she allowed her head to slump back, her eyes to close.

She was nervous. But she was glad at last to be doing something definite. And as the train speeded up as it flew through the southern fields, as brown and dry as the Cumbrian fells with the drought, she combed her hair, rearranged the papers, and prepared to meet her opponent.

She was not ready for the long walk she was faced with when she got off the train. Amy liked walking—but she liked it on gentle grass, with the bleat of lambs around her, and the occasional call of an eagle in the crags above. Not this . . . She straightened her shoulders, neat in the simple linen dress, and reminded herself that this was war, a dangerous mission, and she was not expected to feel comfortable. She was taking the action into the enemy camp. She marched with determination down a ramp marked 'Taxis', only to find a long queue, which rather deflated her original fervour. She stood patiently grasping the precious briefcase. When it finally came to her turn for a cab, two youths leapt over the barrier and took it from her. Still patiently, she waited for the next vehicle to roll down the dirty line towards her. 'Harley Street, please.' She had checked the map, and it didn't seem far.

71

She had intended to take another look at her papers in the taxi, but the impact of the city was too strong—such bustle and rush, such impatience, such dreadful smells! But slowly she began to see names of streets she had only heard of—Marylebone Road, Regents Park. She stared, fascinated, wondering what all these people were doing, rushing round in all directions as though all on important missions like herself. 'Oxford Circus is down there,' the cabbie pointed.

'I hope you aren't taking me a long way round. I'm in a hurry,' Amy said sharply.

'Lor' love you, there's no point in going straight —traffic jams all the way. It'd take hours!' The cabbie smiled at her in the mirror.

'If you say so.' But she watched the meter, clocking up pounds at an alarming speed.

'What number?' he asked at last.

'What?'

'We're 'ere—'Arley Street.'

'Oh.' Amy hastily gave him the number, put her unread notes back in her case, and began to take an interest in the elegant terraces. She had arrived to face her foe. She must be totally on her guard now. Yet she found a sudden sense of pleasure, a frisson of excitement to be standing now outside the very rooms where her handsome sailing partner presided as the august 'C. J. F. MacFarlane, MRCP'. It was polished to a high degree of reflection. She could see her face in it—a trifle pale, her brown hair framing the solemn green eyes, the determined little mouth and chin. She must forget her fragile appearance now. She was about to fire the first broadside . . .

She had wanted to look businesslike but not severe, and the pale green linen served the purpose, being clean-cut, with small sleeves and a simple round neckline. She was fairly certain she didn't look like a country cousin. Yet there wasn't much she could do with her hair, except brush it back and hope it stayed there. She reached up and rang the Victorian bell. No one came.

The traffic roared past. Amy stood, deciding that no one could hear a bell in this noise. But just as she stepped forward to ring again, the large Georgian door was opened, and a petite receptionist stood on the top step, her eyes heavily made up, her white overall crisp and spotless. She gave an insincere smile and said, 'Miss Taggart?'

Amy faced her, remembering she was on campaign. 'Sister Taggart, yes.' That was her fighting name. And to everyone else she knew she was Amy. Never mind the Miss! All the same, she answered the girl's frigid smile with a similar one, and began to climb the stone steps.

'Dr MacFarlane wasn't sure when you would be coming.' As Amy followed her in the girl said, 'I'm Toni. Chris—Dr MacFarlane—has told me what a lovely place you come from.'

'Really?'

Toni accepted the cool tone, though she couldn't know that it was sheer stage fright that was making Amy's speech taut and difficult. 'I'll just tell him you're here.' She tapped off, her elegant heels on the parquet floor seeming to go on for miles once she had left the room. The ceilings were very high, higher than at the Manor, and the mouldings were picked out in Wedgwood blue and silver—unlike at the Manor, where a simple coat of white covered the carvings.

Ah well, she was on his territory now, and she mustn't let it awe her. She must remember him in his white jeans and tee-shirt, steering the *Speedwell* with the light of pure enjoyment in the keen blue eyes. She looked up at the grandfather clock, shining and polished like the brass nameplate. She waited five minutes—ten. Never had minutes been so long. And then suddenly there was no time to collect herself as the door was flung open and Chris was there in person. Amy jumped up like a frightened fawn, scattering her handbag and her briefcase.

Furious with herself for her clumsiness, she looked up into his face, feverishly reminding herself of the casual image she had been remembering. But it was impossible. He stood, even taller than she remembered, in dark grey expensive suit, with waistcoat and dark grey tie with thin red stripes. No one could be more different than the casual-haired youth she had tried to recall. He was not smiling.

For a moment they faced each other. Amy looked into those sky blue eyes, waiting for a sign from him as to what attitude she should take—friendly, or purely businesslike? He held out his firm hand, those long fingers she remembered well. 'Glad you came, Amy.'

She replied with a firm handshake and, 'Glad to be here.'

'You mean that?' And as she nodded, he smiled suddenly and said, 'Good. Because I've just seen off my last patient of the day.'

'But it's only just after two.' She had been glued to the grandfather clock—she knew.

'Well, this is business, isn't it? If Greyrigg isn't worth postponing two or three wealthy neurotics, I don't know who is.'

'I suppose that's fair. Unless it's tactics.'

A touch of a smile lit his eyes as he said, 'Amy Taggart, this isn't a war.'

She felt herself flushing, and looked down at the expensive blue carpet. 'Sorry if I said the wrong thing.' She bent to pick up her case, but Chris was quicker, picking up the file and putting it neatly in the case. She held out her hand.

'I might as well carry this. It is for me, isn't it?' The stern look was back. 'Have you had lunch?'

'No. But I'm not hungry.'

'Okay, then let's go.' Chris ushered her in front of him to a different entrance, down some steps into the sunshine, where his car was waiting. He threw his jacket into the back seat, undid his waistcoat, and took off his tie. Then he opened the passenger door for Amy. 'I thought we'd better go somewhere quiet to talk. Don't worry about the heat.' Inside the car was stifling. 'The air-conditioning will soon take care of that.' The trouble was, the air-conditioning also took care of conversation, as it whirred rather noisily. Amy sat and felt apprehensive as she sat beside the young physician, wondering just how she could regain the initiative.

He drove to a park. There were few people about, and he led the way into a rose garden, with a few benches, and an elderly gardener hoeing between the rose plants, chipping away at the hard dusty soil. On a bench he placed a tray, and a box he took from the boot of the car, and Amy found herself with a glass of wine in her hand, and a smoked salmon sandwich on a napkin beside her. 'It's Chablis—you prefer it, don't you?'

'Yes. It's lovely and cool.' Still she could not think of anything original or sparkling to say to him. He must be very bored, having to spend the afternoon with a country girl, talking about Greyrigg Manor, a place he had never even seen until July. 'I'd like you to read the report before I go back. Unless you want me to leave it with you?'

'I will. You aren't going back right away, are you?'

'I did want to get the evening train.'

'I won't hear of it—you'll be exhausted! There's no problem about accommodation. Now, tell me something about our guests. When is Major Hendon going in for his new hip?'

'I'm going to see about it next Monday,' Amy told him.

'And how's Aggie? And what about that birth certificate? Any sign of it?'

Amy had to smile. 'No. But Sarah-Jane is sure you'll do something about it for her. You captured her heart all right, kissing her hand like that.'

'I did?' Chris caught her eyes and held them with his gaze. 'Hmm.' Then he picked up his glass again, and said, 'Well, Amy, are we friends?'

She had started to relax. 'Friends,' she said, lifting her own glass to him. Then she said, 'If you really are interested in our guests, poor Edna Bell has had a left hemiparesis. But she was coming home today, and Sharla's going to look after her.'

He pulled the hamper towards him on the ground and put his feet on it, leaning back, basking in the sun. Amy averted her eyes from his body, firm and obvious through the thin white silk shirt. 'If anyone can help, Sharla can,' he agreed. 'She thrives on problems like that.'

'I can see that. Chris, why is she so unhappy? I know she's getting a divorce, but surely that means her troubles are over—or almost? She's quite an unhappy person except when she's working.'

Chris's face was grave. 'Her husband married her for her model girl looks, but Sharla isn't that sort of woman. She's a homemaker. She didn't want to go out to night-clubs and such things, like Ray did, and they quarrelled a lot. Then, stupidly, she stopped taking the pill, thinking a child would bring them together. Ray went off. And Sharla turned into a single parent with post-natal depression.'

'Oh no!' Amy's gentle heart went out to her. 'Where's the baby now?'

'With an aunt in Southall. Lovely little girl, she is. But Sharla has to prove that she's mentally stable before she can have her back.'

Amy said quickly, 'But we could have the child with us. There's lots of people to help. And the village school isn't bad. And poor Sharla would be happier instead of going to her room and crying at night.'

Chris didn't answer, and as she looked up, she saw that he was looking at her in a very special way, his eyes full of meaning, if only she could learn to read them. 'Thank you for that.' He drained his wineglass.

'And it would be lovely to have a child about the place. Hannah has a daughter, but she lives in the village, and doesn't come up to the Manor much.'

Chris took a deep breath. 'Now, Amy, we'll both fall asleep in the sun if we sit here. Wait while I put the things in the car, and we'll take a walk in the shady part of the park to wake us up a little.'

'I ought to see about trains home.' But her voice was not insistent. She didn't really want to rush off. Yet she wasn't sure why, except that she hadn't yet floored Chris MacFarlane with the force of her arguments against change at the Manor.

'Toni will do that for you. And she'll ring and let them know to send someone to meet you at Carlisle. Leave that to me. We have other things to talk about.'

They walked slowly along the well-kept paths. Amy said, 'I want you to read what I've written. I want to discuss the points with you.'

'Right.' Suddenly Chris was stalling no longer. They sat in a shady place while he took out the report and skimmed through the headings, stopping here and there to read in more detail. He looked up to see her staring at him, and smiled. 'Amy, don't be so tense! I'm not out to destroy Greyrigg, you know. All I'm concerned with is to make the necessary changes with the least upset to anyone—including the bank manager. Please don't be emotional about it. Let's understand one another. There's work that needs doing.'

'That isn't in dispute. And I'm not emotional.' Her voice rose. 'If you read that properly, you'll see that I've carefully not mentioned anyone's feelings, only staff convenience and patient comfort.'

'I noticed that. Well put.'

'Can we start with the kitchen? I noticed that Quintin had removed all the doors in his sketch, and put arch-ways. He had potted palms around the place, and no sign of the pulley for drying the teacloths.'

Chris said drily, 'Now how on earth did you find that out? He told me his plans were kept locked in his room.'

'It isn't important how I found out, only that you must read what I've written why this is totally impractical. He's never seen Cumbria in winter. He doesn't know anything about condensation, about where the steam goes on a wet day, how we get clothes dry in a hurry, where we keep the extra electric blankets away from damp, how we need all available surfaces for baking and cooking—he's littered them with plants!'

'I take your point.' But in spite of the fair words, his demeanour was less than cordial.

'I suppose you have to accept Quintin's plans to keep well in with Francesca.' The words burst out; Amy had never been good at hiding her feelings. 'I suppose I might have saved my breath and my money. You won't take any notice of me.'

'Hey, wait a minute!' Chris's face was even sterner now, but she didn't care; he had stalled her long enough. He caught her arm and made her face him. 'Didn't you promise that we'd discuss this thing without emotion?'

'I don't call that emotion. I call it common sense in the face of blatant nepotism.'

'Amy!'

'Don't Amy me,' she said crossly. 'It's true, isn't it? You brought him along right from the start, before you'd even seen the Manor—before you even knew that anything needed doing. You never even thought we might have craftsmen and architects in Cumbria, more used to the weather conditions, and better at dealing with them.'

Chris said quietly, 'I brought Sharla Chowdray too. That wasn't wrong, was it? Do you know why? Because you didn't take a dislike to her, as you did to me and to Quintin. Sheer female prejudice. Good lord, woman, I heard you swear you didn't need any further physiotherapy equipment! Yet here you've mapped out an entire new department, which means renovating a broken-down barn and installing heating and lighting!'

So he had at least read the thing properly. 'You may have failed to notice that what I've done is speak to the people concerned, which your precious Quintin thought quite unnecessary,' she pointed out. 'You should have seen him, sneaking around in his baggy breeches and his spiky hair, hiding his notes from us all! Fancy ideas from a fancy idiot, if you ask me. I deal with real people—or maybe you haven't noticed?'

'How could I fail to? You never stop telling me,' said Chris drily.

Amy sat upright, her limbs tense and her face pink with annoyance in the warm afternoon. She was angry with Chris, but even angrier with herself for allowing her anger to show. She deserved to lose the battle she was fighting, if she gave in to childish fury like that. Coolness, a cool head and a calculating brain were the only weapons that had any chance against this powerful enemy.

'Let's go back to the flat,' he said quietly.

They drove back to Harley Street, saying nothing. Amy thought she had never been so miserable in her life, and she didn't know why. She was usually so very sensible when dealing with problems, and rarely lost her temper. She wondered for a little while whether to apologise. But no. If he saw her weaken, he would know he had won. She dared not apologise. But when she saw Chris's face, as tense and anguished as her own, she felt a wave of sympathy for him. It *was* sympathy, wasn't it? She only knew that she blushed hotly when he caught her eye, as they both stood in his well-proportioned living room, and he threw the briefcase on to the coffee table.

He came towards her, and she felt her heart behind her ribs trying to get out. He reached out both hands and took hers gently. 'How about a shower? It's been a hot day.'

'Thank you.'

'We'll go out for a spot of dinner—somewhere quiet. Don't bother to change if you haven't brought anything else. This dress suits you.'

'I've brought another. But I expect your women friends all dress up in the latest fashion? I expect they're all sophisticated and clever.'

He let her hands go, but didn't move away. His voice changed as he tried to explain. 'No, Amy, they aren't any more sophisticated and clever than anyone else. But they *think* they are—that's the difference. And that's why I'd rather be with you.' He turned quickly. 'Your room's in there.' And he went into the other, pulling off his shirt as he went, so that his splendid back caught her eye, though again she tried not to look.

She was in the guest bedroom, with its own shower. She was calmer now, not a bit angry with Chris, and wondering as she stood under the blissfully cool water why they always seemed to strike sparks from each other. He was nice, really. There was no logic in the way she had attacked him earlier. She rubbed herself with a thick luxurious towel, then sat for a while on the bed, wrapped in its comforting softness.

'Amy, you haven't fallen asleep?' Chris stuck his head in. He was already changed into casual shirt and slacks, his hair still a little damp, curling on his neck. Amy looked up, somehow not embarrassed by his presence, though she pulled the towel tighter under her arms. He came in, and knelt by her on the thick carpet. 'You're too tired to go out. I'll fetch something in.' His voice was very gentle now, as though he too felt no embarrassment, as though they were so used to each other that they might have known each other for years. 'What do you say?'

She looked at him, his eyes on a level with hers. And she felt her chin wobble as tears came, and she burst out with, 'I'm such a fool! I shouldn't have spoken to you like that.'

Then she was in his arms, and he was comforting her. And it was a wonderful and heavenly feeling just to forget about everything, and let her head rest on his chest and her tears fall into his towel. Neither of them seemed in a hurry to move. He allowed her to stay within the circle of his arms, holding her tight, stroking her hair, kissing the top of her head lightly, very lightly . . .

She began to speak, feeling calmer now. 'I didn't mean to show you how—how much of a beginner I am at sensible negotiations.'

'No one could have done it better. You fought like a trooper—I'd be made of stone if I didn't see that.'

Very calm now, Amy said, 'I feel better now. Shall we go?'

As though reluctantly, Chris stood up. 'Is this what you're wearing?' Her best chiffon was hanging up, her only other best dress. He had seen the lemon one when he took her to the Meridien.

'Yes. Is it all right?'

'It's nice.'

He went out of the room, and she hurriedly dressed in case he came in again. Her hair was dry, and she gave it a vigorous brushing. She sat in front of the dressing table and took out her little make-up bag, laying out lipstick, eyeshadow and mascara.

A hand came from behind her and covered them so that she couldn't pick them up. 'Don't put that stuff on.' His eyes were soft, his face gentle, and she gazed up at him as though hypnotised by him. 'Just wear your freckles. They suit you.'

He didn't seem to hear when she said she was ready —just kept looking at her as though he couldn't look away. Amy felt herself blushing. He shouldn't do that. She wasn't really used to men, and she didn't know how to deal with him. It wasn't as though he was free. There was the lovely Francesca in his life: she had heard the name from both Quintin and from Sharla. And she had overheard that conversation in his surgery when she was on the phone to him. So there was no doubt about Francesca—and even if Chris could forget her easily, Amy couldn't.

'I'm ready,' she repeated. 'Don't take me anywhere too grand.'

He regained his usual composure. 'All right, we won't do the Ritz tonight. Maybe next time?'

'I'm hoping there won't be a next time.' Amy was able to smile now, easy with him. 'I'm hoping you'll have listened carefully to all my logic and common sense, and will agree not to allow Quintin to vandalise Greyrigg.'

'I'll agree not to do anything in a hurry,' Chris told her.

'Is that all?'

'We'll talk tomorrow—go over every paragraph.'

'But I'm going home tomorrow!' she protested.

'I've arranged for the day after. We need tomorrow for proper negotiations.'

'Do we?'

'Oh yes. I've put off all my engagements tomorrow. You can't walk out on me now.'

'Well, of course I can't, if you're serious. I'd love to spend the day arguing my case.'

'Then it's a date.' He opened the door for her to precede him into the hall. 'Let's go in search of kebabs and Greek bread. It isn't far.'

They walked along the streets in the deepening shadows. Amy felt peaceful now, as though she had come through some sort of initiation. Chris had promised not to do anything in a hurry. So she had won round one, though it had been quite a fight, and she had taken a lot of buffeting. 'I suppose you like Greek food because of your island sailing holidays?'

He didn't seem unwilling to talk of the holidays with Francesca. 'There really is nothing like a good boat, a fair wind, and the green waves all around you. And then in the long warm scented evenings, good company, good food and wine, unspoiled people, goats and olive groves.'

'Why aren't you going this year?' Amy asked.

'I'm spending my holiday seeing to Greyrigg and Four Winds. I find myself rather suddenly with responsibilities.' He guided her down some steps, where a savoury smell beguiled the senses. 'I don't suppose you've seen Four Winds? You said Dad didn't stay there much.'

Amy bit her lip. But the new atmosphere between them made her speak honestly. 'I hadn't seen it last time you came. But I did go along to take a look, last time I took Graham and Peggy to the hospital.' She had not mentioned it to the two old people, but she had made a small detour so that she could see the outside of the house that was once a rather lonely schoolboy's home. 'I thought of you, coming back there in the school holidays in your short trousers and school blazer.'

They were by now sharing a large and succulent lobster, but Chris paused to grin. 'Yes, such I was indeed, many years ago—scruffy and dirty-kneed.' He went on, 'Perhaps that's why Veronica took a dislike to me.'

'Did she really?'

'Probably not. Now that I see it from her point of view, she was just not used to children. And I was probably sullen and hard to manage. I don't expect I was a very nice child, looking back.'

'Perhaps you've made up for it?'

He put down his fork. 'Only perhaps? Aren't you going to tell me I'm the greatest guy you've ever met?'

'There's only one way you can get me to say that,' she told him.

'The Manor?' She nodded. 'I thought so. Amy, short of handing it over to you by deed poll or something, I can hardly have done more!'

She smiled. 'Let's not argue tonight.'

'No, let's hang on to a bit of civility.' They smiled at each other like people who understood one another. And Amy felt a sudden pain in her heart, because she knew that this new and intense feeling she had would mean more hurt and unhappiness later. She seemed tonight to be alert, alive all over. And though unused to men, she knew that it was Chris MacFarlane's doing. She was so happy now, just being with him. The parting pain would be all the more acute. Her mind went back to the words she thought she heard him say over the telephone. Amy, I love you . . . Did she know him well enough to ask if she had heard him right?

'Penny for them?'

She opened her mouth to tell him, but prudence held her back. What was happening to her campaign? One didn't get medals for getting romantic ideas about someone who was already spoken for. 'Are we working in your flat tomorrow?' she asked.

'No way—we'd die of heat exhaustion! No, we'll take a boat up to Oxford . . .'

'We'll what?'

'It's all arranged. Boat to Oxford. Lunch there, and grab a chopper back home. Cool on the water, for careful study of documents—and then quickly back when we've amicably concluded our business.'

The waiter had served them with savoury lamb and peppers. Amy ate, hardly noticing how delicious it was. 'As in helicopter? Are you a millionaire?'

'No. But Dad left me some. And the helicopter belongs to a friend.'

'Don't you think you'll find this a handicap in your negotiations with me? Spending money like water on me, and then shouting at me for wanting a physiotherapy department?'

'I'm not spending the money on you, Amy dear. Only on you as the representative of Greyrigg Manor. You're not a woman now—more of a shop steward, Amy.'

'I see.'

He reached across and squeezed her hand, as though to take away the double-meaning. 'Come on, let's get to bed early, then we can make a flying start.'

Remembering the impassioned embrace of the afternoon, Amy was apprehensive as they climbed the stairs to the back door of the flat. But Chris kept well away, as though regretting his intimacy. 'Good night.' He made for his own room.

She looked after him—and knew she was disappointed that he had not even wanted to kiss her.

CHAPTER SIX

'SHOW a leg, Amy!' Chris was standing beside her bed, with a steaming mug of tea. His lean face was impassive. Amy felt like a nuisance again as she sat up, keeping the duvet pulled up across her naked chest. But there was no need; the moment the cup was in her hands, he was on his way out of the room. 'We'll have breakfast on board,' he said over his shoulder.

She kept reminding herself that staying here had been his idea. She should not think of herself as in his way. Yet she still saw herself as an outsider, an irritating outsider, who had interrupted his nice comfortable world with her insistence on her own way. She drank the tea, fragrant and expensive-tasting. He was treating her nicely, but he was probably wishing he hadn't invited her out for the entire day. Breakfast on board—it sounded so good. But Amy being Amy, she dared not think that Chris might enjoy it too.

And then she began to see the other side. She had come here as a crusader, battling for what Dr Mac had built up. In that light, she felt better. She drank the last sip of tea, showered rapidly, and dressed in the dark blue chiffon of last night. It was light and easy to wear—and from the heat of the rays that were coming in already, it was going to be a scorcher of a day. She put out a hand towards the lipstick—then withdrew. Chris's words had been so lovely, she would remember them always: Wear your freckles—they suit you.

He was really very nice. She had to remind herself that he *had* to be nice to his father's trusted lieutenant. In being nice to Amy, he was showing his father's spirit that he was being faithful to his memory. All the same, some of his remarks she would treasure—Amy saw herself as an old maid, with nothing but memories of what might have been, like Lucy Coats . . .

She went rather hesitantly into the lounge, and tried not to gasp when she saw Chris in his white jeans and blue tee-shirt. There was no way she could be stuffy with him in that outfit. Memories of that hour they had spent sailing together were some of the sweetest she had. 'I'm ready,' she told him.

She still couldn't read his eyes. He was not very chatty. But she hesitated to mention the fact, for fear of being snapped at. But as they left the flat, she said, 'I know I'm a pain in the neck, Chris—but is there any chance of seeing Sharla's baby? I'll be catching the early train tomorrow, and—well, I know she wouldn't mind, honestly.'

'She hasn't told you about Shakira?'

'She wanted to. I know it's all right.'

He turned and faced her. 'Okay, I'll take you to see her—just for a minute or two. It's on the way to the boat. You'll take the responsibility?'

'I will. I love her already.'

Chris seemed to choke back his comments as he led the way down to the car. And he said nothing as they sped through the light early traffic towards the west of London. He seemed to know the way very well. They were soon drawing up in front of a small maisonette, with peeling paint and an overgrown garden. 'Wait—I'll explain who you are.' He ran round to the back door.

The front door opened, and an Indian woman in a white sari edged with maroon came out, with a little girl in her arms. She crossed the untidy lawn, followed by Chris. Her dark eyes were large and suspiciously bright. 'I am second cousin to Sharla's father,' she said. 'The courts gave me custody—they said she was not well enough to look after Shakira.' She paused and said, 'I am very happy to meet a good friend of Sharla.'

Amy looked into the bright black eyes of the little girl, and a lump came into her throat, as she murmured, 'Oh, my dear little thing!' She held out her arms, and Shakira responded with an open trust that thrilled Amy. She took the child in her arms, and could not disguise her emotion. She hugged her against herself, saying to the aunt, 'Could you part with her?'

'Oh yes. We love her, but her place is with her mother. The court was very stupid. And this place is too small for a child to be comfortable.'

Amy thought of the lovely gardens the little girl could grow up in. 'Then we have a deal. Chris will help us, won't he?'

'Dr MacFarlane has done everything.' The black eyes shone with gratitude. 'For everything we have turned to him, and he has helped us with money and with kindness.' The woman took the child back to her breast, and Amy could see it would be hard to give her up.

'You would have to come and visit her often.'

The aunt smiled then, and her tears spilled over. 'God bless you!' she whispered.

There was no conversation in the BMW, as they turned towards Richmond, where the chartered launch was moored. Chris handed over the keys, and the boatman pointed out the elegant craft. 'There's all the food you ordered,' he told them.

'Thanks.' Chris turned to help Amy down, but she was already aboard. They waved, and Chris started the engine.

'Are you pleased that Shakira will be coming to her mother?' Amy asked him.

She expected him to say something happy, but his voice was strained as he said, 'It's probably the best arrangement.' She wondered if he resented his own kindness in the case being known. Perhaps he even was fond of Sharla himself? But that was not on Amy's mind at the point. Only the bright innocent face of Sharla's baby, and excitement that she might come to be the darling of Greyrigg.

She made her way to the galley. 'I'm starving! Time for breakfast. Do you want absolutely everything? Fried bread, the lot?'

He looked down at her, and again the expression of

his handsome face was studiously giving nothing away.
'Let's see what you can do.'

'You must have found out by now that I enjoy a
challenge.' She turned back and examined the contents
of the locker and the fridge. Yes, she could give him
a fairly decent five-star breakfast. And as her own
appetite was sharpened by the emotional visit to little
Shakira, she set to her work with vigour. She laid a place
at the table, and prepared fruit juice and cereal, before
beginning to grill sausages and bacon. In no time, a
banquet was ready for the hungry helmsman. Neither of
them said very much, as Chris ate while Amy steered,
and then she had her food, as the sun became hotter.
Chris said, with grudging praise, 'I haven't had a breakfast like that for years.'

'I hope you won't in several more years!' she laughed.
'It's too high in cholesterol.'

'Is there any more toast?'

She brought a plate of toast and marmalade, and
made a second pot of coffee. The atmosphere between
them had thawed, but was still slightly reserved. She
couldn't understand how Chris could be so approach-
able one day, and so unreadable the next. They threw
the crusts to the ducks along the way, attracting the
attention of some magnificent white swans at Marlow.
The river unfolded in the gentle rolling fields and wood-
lands of the Thames Valley. Amy had to admit that it
had a beauty of its own, despite the lack of mountains.

Early in the afternoon Oxford appeared in a blue
heat-haze, the towers and spires as beautiful as Chris
had told her. 'We won't need lunch. I'll moor near a pub
I know, and we'll take the papers with us.' They began to
pass students and young people sunning themselves on
the banks, and the occasional punt, propelled by a
sweating youth, with his maiden sitting idly at the other
end. Amy's face must have shown envy, for Chris called,
'Have you never been in a punt?'

She turned and smiled. 'I've never had a young man to
take me.'

'You make it sound as though it's too late.'

'I'm twenty-eight,' she pointed out.

'Good lord! And I thought you were only eighteen.' He was joking, of course, and Amy was relieved that his standoffish mood had relaxed just a little bit more. 'Can you jump off at that bollard, Amy? The King Edward is only a step away.' They moored and locked the boat, and Amy picked up the file of her notes. Chris took it from her, saying with a crooked smiled, 'This is becoming well travelled.'

'Just so long as it isn't ignored,' she said emphatically, and he raised his eyebrows and begged to be excused from another telling-off.

They strolled along the towpath together but not touching. Amy said, 'I didn't ask to come all this way.'

He turned apologetically. 'I'm sorry—was I rude? I thought this would please you, seeing the Thames valley, and Oxford.'

'It does. But not if you're thinking all the time of the patients you ought to be seeing, or the young lady you ought to have been meeting for lunch.'

'You're sharp with me,' Chris said drily.

'Can we stop and get down to business?'

He looked at the file he was carrying. 'Just another few yards.' And indeed the King Edward was a black and white pub in the very best English tradition. It was restful to go inside, feel the coolness of the slate floor, and taste the fresh taste of chilled lager.

They sat in a shady corner, and Chris opened the file. He turned to her. 'If I give you the go-ahead to do all this, you think you can cope with it?'

'Just try me! I've been at the Manor for six years, Chris. I've coped with everything—helped by your father, of course, who did what you suggested and gave me a free hand. Pity I didn't get a testimonial from him before he died.' She looked up into his face. 'Did you mean it?'

He gave a rueful smile. 'I'm beginning to lose, Amy. I

think I need another beer.'

'I'll get it.' She went over to the bar counter. 'After all, this is a business trip.' And she leaned across and had a word with the cheerful landlord. In a moment, he was back with a bottle of champagne. Amy said, 'This is to say thank you for your hospitality. And—' she sat down, and looked a little shy—'and because I'm thirsty and we both like Veuve Clicquot.'

Chris poured into the glasses the landlord brought, and looked across at Amy. 'There's just so much to you,' he remarked. 'You're always surprising me.'

'I sometimes surprise myself,' she confessed.

'You were—oh, why try to explain a woman? Why not just enjoy being with her?' He held up his glass. 'To Amy Taggart.'

'To me? Oh no!' she protested.

'To the best nagger, the trouble and strife, the tycoon, the retiring violet, the bully, the angel, the freckle-faced urchin and the most beautiful girl in the world.' He drained his glass recklessly, and went on, 'And the winner in our armed struggle. Truce, Amy. I can't fight you any more.'

'Why not?'

'You really don't know?'

She looked at him carefully. The strain in his eyes was showing. 'Just because you've accepted my report, I don't want you to think I'll be stupid about it,' she told him. 'I've got time to do the alterations before the bad weather starts. And we don't have to do everything in one year. I'll plan it out again, Chris, according to what's most urgent, shall I?'

'I trust you, Amy. Go back to your country of fells and lakes, and rule it as you've done in the past.'

She sipped her wine. 'I think I see. You're washing your hands of me. I can't say I blame you. You ought to have let me go home the first night.'

'It isn't anything personal,' he assured her.

'I'm just a hiccup in the orderly running of your life, is that it?'

'More or less.' Chris was smiling now, as the wine relaxed him.

'Tell me about you and Quintin at school?' she invited.

He talked frankly, though in mentioning his holidays at the Forbes residence in Henley, he managed never to mention the beautiful Francesca. When they had finished the wine, they went out into the sunshine, and walked slowly along the river, pushing aside the willows as they walked. Chris's tongue was loosened, as long as he was talking about the past. But when Amy asked a question about the present or the future, he made some excuse, and changed the subject. She at last asked frankly, 'Chris, are you happy in what you do?'

'Yes. My father always wanted me to succeed. What more can I get from life than a large private practice and a good reputation?'

'There may be other things? Did you secretly want to go off to China to be a missionary? Your sense of duty might have led you into success you didn't really want.'

'My dear Amy, if I wanted to be a missionary, I'd get up off my backside and go right ahead and be one,' he assured her.

'Good for you! That's what I'd do too.'

Chris stopped and leaned against a tree trunk, facing her. 'You mean to tell me you're completely and utterly fulfilled, doing what you're doing?'

'Yes.' Then she looked up into his eyes and said, 'Well, qualified fulfilled.'

'Go on.'

Amy sat on the grass and slipped off her sandals, dabbling her feet in the water among the bulrushes. Looking out to the opposite bank as Chris sat beside her and followed her example, she said, 'I had a long talk with Lucy Coats the other night. She thinks I ought—to be settling down. But I'm not sure yet.'

The silence between them was almost tangible. A grasshopper chirped cheekily only inches away. Chris began to speak, then stopped, picking up a pebble and skimming it across the surface of the river. Amy looked up to ask him what he was going to say, and felt his warm breath on her cheek as he bent his head down so that their heads were close together.

The silence lengthened. Amy felt very sad that they had come so close, yet tomorrow would separate them, never again to reach this warm sense of intimacy. She felt there was so much to say, so much they had in common—and yet there was no point, because their lives were miles apart, and neither of them was likely to want to change.

Chris said after a while, 'I've brought you to Oxford, Amy. Would you like to see some of the city?'

'Very much.'

They walked together into the town, pausing to look into the shop windows, many of them strange and exotic to Amy, who kept wanting to buy souvenirs, but was prevented by Chris, 'Wait till we get to the High,' he told her.

He showed her the ancient colleges, their mellow stone beautiful in the sun, their towers clear against a sky the colour of Chris's eyes. 'That's Christ Church,' he said.

Amy stopped, her heart tugged. 'Graham Bell was here.' They walked inside the great quadrangle, her mind a jumble of thoughts and regrets, both hers and her friends back at the Manor. Graham and Edna had never asked to go back. But to have lived in a place like this—surely they must miss it. 'I must buy a postcard at least,' she decided.

'We'll go to the shops.'

They were standing by an old arched gateway looking at the postcards Amy had bought, when there was a shout—a woman's voice, very close to them. They both looked up.

'Christopher!'

A very trendy lady with a long flowing skirt, and hair to match, her make-up striking as a *Vogue* model's, was crossing the street towards them. She gazed up at Chris as though he were the only man in the world. 'What are you doing here, my only love? Fallen from heaven in answer to my prayers? Why aren't you working?'

Chris was embarrassed but polite. 'Hi, Fran. I'm working. This is my—er—colleague from the Manor in the Lakes. She's here on business. Amy, this is Quintin's sister Francesca.'

'Hello, Amy.' Francesca gave her a brilliant smile that reminded her of an iceberg hit by a sunbeam—cold at heart. 'You know my good-for-nothing brother, then?'

'Not well,' Amy answered.

Fran smiled again. 'You really ought not to monopolise this hot property. He's much in demand, you know.'

'Don't worry,' Amy said stolidly, 'I'm going back tomorrow.'

'Are you staying with Chris?'

Amy was capable of handling her. 'If you'll excuse me a moment, there's something in that little craft shop I'd love to take back to my old ladies.' And she swept across the road with as much aplomb as Francesca had shown as she arrived. Hot property? Yes, Chris was an eligible bachelor all right—the best with enough kindness and humanity in him to match his good looks and pleasant nature.

She looked through the shop window. Francesca was holding on to Chris's hand. Those long fingers that had once been enmeshed in Amy's hair . . . She picked up a Chinese vase, her eyes suddenly blurred with tears. Why had Chris made her stay on? Did he know she would fall for him? Did he think he could get his own way by making her fall for him? Yet it hadn't worked; he'd given in. She put the vase down before she dropped it, and waited for her emotions to calm down before buying a wooden carving of a Japanese god with a big tummy.

Chris was at the door. Francesca had gone. 'You took a long time choosing,' he observed.

'I didn't want to be a gooseberry,' Amy explained.

'She has no claim on me.'

Their eyes met, and she wondered if he had any idea

of the overwhelming physical pressure on her, as she felt herself pulled towards him as though by a magnetic force. She murmured, 'I'm sorry, I had no right to say that.'

'You've said plenty of other things you shouldn't have said.' His eyes were smiling now. 'Don't worry, I can take it.'

'Poor thing! But you did bring it on yourself, inviting me,' she pointed out.

'At least we've sorted things out.'

'Yes. I'm very grateful, Chris.'

'That's okay. Now, let's hit the road. I ordered the chopper for five-thirty.' They wound their way through some fascinating little side streets, the creamy yellow college walls shining like fairytale castles in the sunlight. It would have been nice to stay on. But Amy was feeling uncomfortable with him now, knowing he had been generous with his time, and feeling he must want to be rid of her. A small helicopter was waiting in a meadow by the river, the rotors spinning slowly. They ran across to it, bending to avoid the wind made by the blades, and Chris introduced Amy to the pilot. 'How are you, Alan?' he asked.

'Can't grumble; all the Arabs who like to go from A to B in a hurry!' Alan lifted the machine off the ground, and said politely, 'Where are you from, Amy?'

'Daweswater.'

'I say, I've heard of that. My old Prof—Graham Bell—went to live there.'

'You have a degree in social sciences, then?' Amy explained how she knew.

'Tell him that Alan Price sends his kindest regards.' He circled the town. 'Look down there—can you see where the motorway comes into the town? That's the M40. Now, we go along in that direction. I'll point out any landmarks.' Amy stared, fascinated. They seemed to be flying over a map. It took only a very short time to get back to the centre of London, that had taken so many hours by boat.

They walked back along the streets instead of taking a cab. The sun was low now, most buildings in shadow. Amy said, 'I feel rather inadequate saying thank you. It's been such an experience.'

'I'm glad,' smiled Chris.

'Sorry to be such a troublesome business associate.'

'I was only joking. I could handle you if I wanted.' He put a hand on her shoulder, and left it there after a gentle squeeze.

'What shall I say to Quintin?' Amy asked.

'Nothing. Let him play along for a few more weeks. He's got more money than he knows what to do with. He won't lose by not getting the work. And it keeps him happy.'

They reached the stairs to the flat. Chris fumbled for his key and let them in. They sat for a while in silence, listening to the distant hum and bustle of the never-ending traffic. 'What are you thinking, Amy?' he asked.

'That it will be quieter at home.'

'You don't like London?'

'It's exciting, but it isn't real living—not for me.'

'So you don't want to find another glamorous eating spot?'

She sat up and shook her head. 'I couldn't take it.'

He laughed. 'Go and take a shower. I'll grab something from the fridge.'

Amy obeyed, standing at the door of the bedroom and looking back at him stretched out in an armchair. She smiled into his eyes, and for a moment wanted to go back and kneel at his feet and kiss his tired eyes, but she turned quickly, resisting the idea.

She came back in her cotton housecoat. Chris had placed a tray with two pizzas and a fresh salad on the coffee table, and was just mixing two dry Martinis. She smiled, 'This is paradise!'

He handed her a Martini. 'I hope you give me the same treatment when I come to Greyrigg. Including that breakfast!'

'Don't you prefer to stay at the Meridien?'

'No. The Manor.' He met her eyes, and toasted her silently before sipping his drink.

'Let me know in time, then I can stock up on caviare.'

He smiled again. 'I hate caviare.'

'So do I. What do you like?'

'Maybe we could take *Speedwell* out and catch something ourselves? Trout, maybe, or roach? I'd like that . . .' his voice trailed away, as though he could see the sunlit lake in his mind's eye.

Amy felt choked suddenly. How long would she wait for him to come again to the Manor? Far better to assume that he would be too busy to make the trip. 'Don't expect sunshine next time,' she warned. 'This summer has been a one-off.'

'It has indeed, Amy Taggart . . .'

Silence fell. They ate, without much enthusiasm, then Chris went out to put some coffee on.

The telephone rang. Chris went to answer it in the hall, and Amy tried her best not to listen. Tense, she knew it must be a woman—probably the girl they had met this afternoon. Occasional words came through the door, which was just ajar. 'For goodness' sake, woman, take it easy! That's no way to speak to the man of your dreams . . . Yes, there sure is a threat . . . no, I can't say anything else . . . that sort of language is unbecoming, darling. Yes, all right . . . sure, I'll be there . . .'

He came back. 'Well, back to your friends tomorrow, Amy? You're lucky, having such a big family. You're good to them, I know, but they fulfil a need for you too.'

'Yes, I see that,' she agreed.

'My patients are my superiors—they pay me as they would pay a servant, you know.'

'I get paid too. But there's more of a relationship at Greyrigg.' She chatted so that she would not be tempted to ask questions about the phone call.

'Relationship—good word.' Chris came across and sat on the arm of her chair. She tensed again as he touched her cheek, wound his fingers in a curl of her hair. Looking straight ahead, and keeping strictly still, she said, 'I think I'll turn in, Chris.'

He looked down at her, and she faced him nervously. He said gently, 'I would if I were you, Amy Taggart.'

Amy lay in the comfortable double bed looking up at the ceiling, her body tense with—with what? She should be delighted, having gained from Chris MacFarlane exactly what she had come for—his approval for her to run the Manor as she chose, and the right to veto any of Quintin's plans she thought unsuitable. Yet she lay in an agony of doubt—had she offended him permanently? He had said so very little—yet he had insisted on her staying for the two nights. She ought not to have agreed.

She heard Chris moving about in the lounge, maybe putting the glasses in the kitchen, straightening the cushions . . . He had given up his time to take her out and give her a treat. She had enjoyed it very much. Yet she didn't feel happy. Somehow in winning the battle, she had made Chris unhappy, and that was the last thing she wanted. For all his difference from her, his lack of sympathy with her way of life, she still hoped for a better rapport between them. She had tried hard to be friendly that day. Yet now she lay, alert and wakeful, feeling that she had failed.

Suddenly she heard the whisper of her door being opened, pushing softly against the thick pile of the Indian carpet. And her body reacted in a way that scared her, feeling languid yet taut, yearning towards him in a way she had never experienced before with any man. He moved on bare feet towards the bed. 'Are you asleep, Amy?' he whispered.

She was going to pretend, but it was no good—her eyelids would not stay closed. She rolled over, and pulled the duvet up, in spite of the heat. Chris was going to make love to her. She felt the atmosphere between them, electric, charged with emotion, with love and fear and longing. And then something happened. She decided it was all right. Her limbs relaxed, and she looked up, facing him with trust and sincerity. 'I almost was,' she told him.

He sat on the very bottom of the bed. 'I just remembered—about Sharla. I wanted to remind you not to mention Shakira unless she does. She'd think I'd let her down, taking you there.'

Amy swallowed, feeling herself blushing in reaction to her previous expectations. 'I won't. But you will go ahead and make the first move in her being re-assessed?' Chris nodded, patted her feet, and left the room.

CHAPTER SEVEN

AMY sat in the window seat, jolting back to Cumbria and
reality in stupendous heat. She felt as though she had
never stopped feeling embarrassed since last night. In
her twenty-ninth year of life, she had suddenly found out
what it was to be aroused physically, to desire someone.
It was so overwhelming that she had no inclination to
look at the newspaper Chris had bought her at Euston,
no will to make plans for the Manor, no wish to go home
. . . The briefcase lay on the luggage rack, the file
unread. It had suddenly achieved a position of being
totally uninteresting to Amy. That too bewildered her,
made her try hard to think what had really happened to
bring this state of things about.

She had not really done or said anything to give herself
away—that was one consolation. She wiped her forehead, and looked out of the window at the parched
southern meadows. What had Chris said as they parted?
So very little. And she had been too frightened to say
anything, in case she betrayed her inner passions, so
abruptly discovered. He had wished her a safe journey
and she had thanked him for the lift to the station. She
closed her eyes, seeing again his tall form in the grey
professional suit, striding away without looking back.

He didn't give tuppence for Amy Taggart. That was
the dreadful truth. He had to be nice to her, as they were
so closely connected with the Manor, but he still hank-
ered after his former, more uncomplicated life. She
could tell. Why else should he look so preoccupied when
they were together? And being a realist, although a
realist in love, she knew she would have to come to terms
with the painful truth.

She had kept her eyes closed, hoping for sleep, but
when they reached Carlisle she felt as though she had

99

walked all the way, so tired yet alert did she feel. She walked along the platform, so much shorter than Euston. She had been away for two nights only, but two nights that had changed her profoundly. 'Hello, Amy? No need to rush. I've got the Land Rover outside.'

'Oh, Larry! I didn't realise I was hurrying. How did you know I'd be on this train?'

'Chris rang me,' Larry told her.

'Oh.'

'He's a thoughtful chap. I like him—and to be honest, I didn't think I would when we first met.'

No chance of keeping him out of the conversation, then. 'No. He's been sensible about the Manor, too. I can go ahead with the insulation and the barn.'

'That's great! Sharla will be delighted.' Larry guided her to the kerb where he was parked. 'We had our first ballroom dancing session last night. She wanted me there, to make sure nobody danced without my okay.'

An idea began forming in Amy's head. Sharla was settling down wonderfully. She would soon know the patients as well as Amy did. Amy could retire from the Manor, as she had first wanted to after Dr Mac's death. Sharla would make an admirable Warden-in-Charge. Amy was cheered by this escape route she had just decided on. It would make her life easier to cope with, if she had the aim of finding another job to think about.

'How's Edna?' she asked.

'She's home, and cheerful. We're full of hopes.'

Larry drove quickly back the thirty miles to Daweswater. The countryside was dry, but the purple fells and the bracken, the sheep and the blue sky, lifted Amy's heart and spirits. And as they rounded the lake, and turned up the last few yards from the village to Greyrigg, she found herself on the edge of the seat looking out for the familiar grey stone walls, the Virginia creeper, and the yellow roses round the portico.

There was nobody about. Afternoon rests should be over, but the Manor was very quiet. Amy ran in, dumped her case in the office, and looked around for

Sharla, Olive or Daniel. 'Hello? Anyone home?' she called.

Olive appeared at the top of the stairs. 'Oh, Amy, is Dr Ford with you? We've got an outbreak of sickness and diarrhoea—Sharla thinks it might be salmonella. We've rung the Health people to take samples. Could you ask Dr Ford to come up?'

Larry was right behind Amy. He loped up the stairs two at a time, while Amy followed more slowly. They went into the first bedroom, Aggie Brown's. The poor little thing lay, deathly white, a bowl beside her, holding her arms across an obviously painful stomach. Larry went into action at once. Amy stood back as he went from room to room. Sharla was with Edna and Graham, who were not in bed, just sitting in their room. 'We didn't have the ice-cream this morning,' they told him.

'It was ice-cream? But Gwyn makes her own.'

Sharla came in, her pretty hair dishevelled. 'It was my fault. A van came round—and we were all so very hot.'

'Are you ill too?' asked Chris.

'I was sick, but I'm okay now. I only had a small one. But some of them had big cones, and three or four had two, and they're the worst, Amy. I'm wondering if we can cope with them here. They may need IV drips.'

Gwyn Jones' dumpy little form appeared at the foot of the staircase. 'Can you tell me if anyone needs an evening meal, or are they all on boiled water and sugar?' she asked.

'I'll let you know in a few minutes, when Dr Ford has finished.' Amy sighed, wondering if she would have made the same mistake if she were in charge instead of Sharla. 'I suppose standards of hygiene must be slipping because people are trying to save water.' She sat down on a chair in Sarah-Jane Phelps' room. Thank goodness Sarah-Jane had decided not to have ice-cream. Amy felt suddenly very tired. But there was no time for rest when the guests needed her. She dragged herself round with Larry, and made sure all the healthy ones were rounded up in the dining room, and provided with supper.

'Me? I really couldn't eat a thing.' She was waiting to go to bed, waiting for blessed sleep to come, and with any luck blot out the events of the past few days. Her eyelids were heavy, but she felt guilty leaving them until there really was nothing else she could do.

She was in her room that evening. It was about nine o'clock, and she was grateful for a comparatively early night. And then the phone rang. Sharla was in the office, and had put the call through. 'It's a Sister Hall from Heaton Grange.' Heaton Grange was a council-run home. Amy knew Dandy Hall—nice woman.

'Hello, Dandy?'

'I'm glad I've caught you, Amy. I've just had the news that we're closing—not yet, of course, but within the year. How many spare beds have you?'

'Two. But as we're in the middle of an outbreak of salmonella—at least that's what it seems to be—can we postpone this conversation until it's over?'

'Oh, my goodness! Sorry, Amy. Yes, I'll leave you to get on with it, love. But please remember us—I've got six months to place my people, then it will be curtains for the Grange. Be in touch.'

Amy tried to think. They had two rooms vacant, but if Dandy Hall were very stuck, they could utilise a staff bedroom—Hannah and Olive didn't live in, and there was a spare. There was also the barn. If that had proper heating and washing facilities, it was possible to turn the loft into at least two bedrooms . . . Her active mind was again dwelling on other people's problems, as a way of forgetting her own . . .

There was a tap on the door. It was Olive. 'Amy, Doris Owens is really ill. She didn't have much ice-cream, so it might not be the food poisoning thing, but she says she's in terrible pain.'

Amy flung on her cotton housecoat and went along to Doris's room. Doris was a retired schoolteacher, tough and uncomplaining as a rule, but her pleasant round face was contorted as she clutched at her stomach. Even when obediently lying flat for Amy to examine her, she moaned with the pain. Amy felt her tummy carefully. 'This seems more like gall bladder to me. Doris, didn't Dr Ford prescribe some stomach medicine for you about three months ago?'

'Yes. Said it might be a hiatus hernia.'

'Did it help?'

'Yes, it did.'

'And where is it now?'

It was Olive who answered. 'It's finished, Amy. We threw the empty bottle out last week, and we forgot to order more.'

Amy looked down at the sorry form on the bed, bent and patted Doris's hand. 'I'll give the chemist a ring—he doesn't go to bed before eleven. After that we'd have to take you to the AED. Hold on, Doris, we'll get your medicine.'

She directed Olive to give Doris some milk. 'But watch that no one with food poisoning has anything but boiled water, won't you, Olive?'

Amy looked in vain for Arthur Taylor. He must have gone home to his cottage along the road. Amy undressed, pulled on her jeans and a thin sweater, and went downstairs. She rang Mr King first, and told him what it was she needed. 'It was thoughtless of me to let stocks get so low.'

'No bother, Amy love, we weren't in bed. I'll go down and get it if you'll come round to the side door. Or would you like me to come out?'

'No, no.' Amy couldn't let him come; it wasn't an emergency. 'I've got the Ford at the door.'

That wasn't exactly true, but it only took seconds for her to back the little estate out of the barn, and drive along the lake shore, headlights blazing towards Kilderton. The night was beautiful, as she got out of the car at the chemist's back door. He was waiting for her. 'Let me know when she's nearly finished the bottle,' he said.

'I will. But if she's going to be seriously ill, she'll need a specialist.'

'You're out of breath, lass. Take it easy now.'

Amy opened the car windows wide on the way back, both for the welcome breeze and for the calming influence of the lake, still and kind, with just a few gentle ripples she could hear lapping under the overhanging grasses. She breathed deeply the fresh lakeside air, emptying her lungs of the polluted city fumes, and trying with the clean air to empty her mind of the unsettling young physician she had left there, striding away from her as she turned to wave . . .

It was midnight when she got back, and most of the guests were asleep. Doris was still awake, but her pain had lessened, and she took a spoonful of the antacid gratefully. Amy walked up to her room in the great silent house. It had been quite a homecoming! But she was glad to be back. Perhaps with time Chris would fade from her thoughts, as no doubt she already had faded from his.

She heard moaning in the night—George Bridges, probably. She heard Daniel go to him. They had the appropriate painkillers. She got up again, as Daniel was not qualified to give an intravenous injection.

When she woke, it was late, the sun high in the morning sky. No wonder! She had slept a long almost undreaming sleep, and felt refreshed, glad it was Sunday. She usually took the mini-bus to church, as several of the guests liked to go, but today the after-effects of the sickness made the mini-bus redundant, and after running to get the papers, she showered and dressed, then walked back again into Daweswater village just as the old cracked bell was beginning to peal for Matins.

'I say, you don't mind if I join you?'

She swung round. Surely Quintin didn't want to come to church? But he did. 'Glad to have your company,' she said politely.

He smiled. 'I think we get on better than we did, don't you?'

Amy smiled too, responding to his overtures of reconciliation. 'Perhaps we just understand one another?'

After the service it became clear why Quintin had

tagged along. The strains of the organ voluntary could still be heard along the quiet, dusty road, with the scent of roses from round the cottage doors making the hot air heavy with sweetness. He said, 'I hear you met my sister?'

'Francesca? Yes. Did she ring you?'

'Last night. She said you were very sweet and natural. I had to agree with her, hadn't I?' He was trying to be nice, and Amy wondered why.

She privately considered Francesca's remarks to be a cruelly artful way of saying that she was naïve and countrified. However, she merely said, 'As I said, we understand one another, Quintin. She thought I was boring.'

'She was surprised to see you with Chris. He's usually a workaholic—no one can tempt him away from his practice on weekdays.'

He was trying to find out how close Amy and Chris were—on Fran's orders! It was transparent now. And she smiled inside, intending to keep them guessing. It was very flattering for such a beauty as Francesca to be jealous of Amy Taggart.

'Ah, well, we were on business,' she explained.

'But why go to Oxford on business?'

'Quite simple—I'd never been there.'

'I don't see that. There was no reason . . . He didn't take you to the Lawsons' place, did he?' Quintin looked worried. 'That wasn't one of my more sophisticated efforts. I've learned a lot since the Lawsons.'

Amy was beginning to enjoy herself. 'Quintin, does Fran care a lot about Chris?' she asked.

'I wouldn't know. She's all over the place with different fellows—part of the job, when you're a model as much in demand as she is.' Quintin was offhand, but Amy was convinced that Fran regarded her as a rival. 'We both like Chris a lot. We've been friends for a long time.'

'Well, I haven't got that advantage. If you count up, Quintin, I've only met the good doctor on a couple of occasions. Hardly time to get to know each other really, is it?' And she smiled again, and waited for his comments.

'It all depends what you got up to on those couple of occasions.'

Amy stopped. They were almost at the Manor gates, and Nell was trotting along to meet them, her tail high and her tongue out. Amy said sweetly, 'And that's something not even a boring country girl goes talking about.' And she ran ahead of him, calling to Nell, and picking a stick to fling as far across the meadow as she could. Let Quintin make of that what he wanted.

Quintin followed slowly, his hands thrust deep in the pockets of his baggy pants, giving him a touch of Charlie Chaplin. But he caught her up before she got to the portico. 'I say, I'm pleased we can make a start on the roof,' he said. 'Did Chris say which plans for the barn he likes?'

Amy felt a surge of delight as she was able to turn and say, 'He left it entirely to me, Quintin. Shall we make a date to go over yours this afternoon?'

Quintin's face was a study. Then he said cheerily, 'Fair enough,' and ran upstairs to his room. Amy heard the door slam, and hugged herself. Good old Chris! He had given her the freedom she wanted. The price for this freedom appeared to be the loss of her heart—but no doubt she would get over it. She still felt highly pleased with herself, as she pulled out her own suggestions about the barn. Surely between them, with Sharla as adviser, seeing that she would be spending most time in the place, they could turn the barn into a very creditable annexe to the Manor. The telephone rang at her elbow, and she sang into it, 'Hello? Greyrigg Manor?'

'You sound well and happy, Amy Taggart.'

'Oh—Chris.' For a moment she felt as though she had been winded. Then she quickly pulled herself together. 'Yes, I am.'

'Glad to be back?'

'Oh yes. Apart from a mild outbreak of salmonella, everything's fine.'

'You're joking?'

'No. But it's almost over now.'

She waited. Chris said slowly, 'I just rang to see what you intend to start doing first.'

'We're having a meeting this afternoon,' she told him. 'Quintin and Sharla and me.'

'Would it be too much trouble to ask you to keep me up to date with the improvements?'

Amy stopped being on her guard. 'Of course I will, you know that. I'm so truly grateful to you for giving us the go-ahead. I promise you'll be told everything we do—I'm sorry if I didn't sound grateful when I left you. I was awfully tired and rather overwhelmed by all your—kindness——'

'Has Sharla mentioned the baby yet?' he asked.

'There hasn't been time.'

'Okay. So long as you let me know.' He paused. 'Are you sailing this week?'

'I'm not planning to—we're going to be busy with ideas and meetings and things.'

'I suppose even meetings are pleasant in that place?'

'Don't tell me you hanker after the country? You can get out to Berkshire and Oxford so easily.'

'There are no mountains!' He was copying her own complaint, but laughingly. ''Bye, Amy.'

She sat, immobilised by the power of his presence. Now that she had seen his flat, she knew just where he was sitting, in the armchair by the grey extension phone. She opened her mouth to say goodbye. And then, in the background, she heard the unmistakable sound of a female voice. Her 'goodbye' turned into a strangled squeak, and she put the phone down with a bang. So Francesca was there too—probably cooking lunch for him. She really must stop seeing him as having anything in common with herself. He led a totally foreign life, he was completely tied up with his city friends, and in the words of the poet, 'Never the twain shall meet.'

After lunch, which they had in the dining room as it was Sunday, and half the guests still did not feel like eating, Amy felt sleepy. But the windows were wide open, and the sound of the sheep and the birds came in happily, together with the bumble-bees, droning and bumping along under the roses.

Quintin was ready, his files under his arm. 'You're a clever little body, Amy, I must agree. But there are things here which you won't understand, so we'll have to take it step by step.'

'Right, O wise one. I'll go and find Sharla.'

'Where shall we work?'

'We could start off in the garden, so we can walk across to the barn if necessary.'

'Right, I'll wait for you there.'

Sharla was in her room, and there were tears on her cheeks. She looked embarrassed when Amy popped her head round the door. Amy said quickly, 'I don't want to pry. If you want to be alone, just say so. But we're starting to redesign the barn, and we thought you'd like to be in on it.'

Sharla hastily wiped her face. 'I do, Amy. It will do me good.'

'That ex-husband of yours has a lot to answer for.' Amy kept her voice casual, but Sharla seemed to be glad she had brought the subject up.

'It isn't really his fault. There were mistakes on both sides. There's no such thing as being all black or all white. I can't blame Ray. I blame my own ignorance of men, really. It was foolish to marry in all the first flush of love, without knowing each other properly.'

'You certainly learned the hard way,' remarked Amy.

'I've learned. No more men for me.'

'That's a bit drastic, Sharla.' But to a certain extent, Amy felt the same. This love business was treacherous. No wonder they said that the god of love was blind! He made humans fall for the most unsuitable people . . . Amy sat on the bed as Sharla brushed her hair. 'Want to talk?' she asked.

'Maybe later . . .'

They passed Sarah-Jane and Damaris arguing in the garden. Sarah-Jane was making quite a fuss, when she was told that no one had done anything about finding her birth certificate. Damaris, her pretty head, sparrow-like, cocked on one side, pointed out that the birthday was months away. 'We've got to have autumn yet, old lass, then Christmas, and then most of the winter before there's any need to worry. February the fourteenth is ages away. Anyway, what difference does a telegram from the Queen matter? You'd be better off being nice to your friends at Greyrigg, or you might find yourself with nowt!'

The Major was more understanding of Miss Phelps' preoccupation. 'The Queen is a symbol, Damaris. Her Majesty and her father before her, and his father before him. They hold the nation together. A telegram symbolises that we're all her family.'

'Pity we have to hit a hundred before she teks any notice!'

The three planners finally made themselves comfort-able around a garden table. Amy soon found out what she had feared—that Quintin's proposed alterations to the barn were too theatrical, too complicated and too expensive. 'It's very artistic, Quintin,' she said tactfully. 'Shall we start at the beginning, and see what must be done first in the way of electricity and repairs to the fabric?' It was going to be a long haul. But it was the way she had wanted it. Amy Taggart didn't quit. She soon realised that the basics would be costly even before they brought in any equipment. 'Never mind, we'll take it one step at a time. If we see to the roof at the same time as the Manor roof, that will be ready before the bad weather. The other things we can take more time over.'

There was a low rumbling noise. Quintin quipped, 'We spoke too soon. The barn is collapsing!' But as they looked around, it slowly dawned on them what the noise was. 'Surely not? It's thunder—real thunder. Shall I give you a hand getting the tables in?'

'But the sky is blue.' All the same, Amy went in search of Arthur Taylor, who was in his favourite spot, com-muning silently with his beehives in the corner of the vegetable garden, his trusty pipe and baccy his only companions. Arthur was delighted. 'I'm fair sick and tired of watering the beans and sprouts. I'll be right glad of a drop of rain.'

Nell seemed to sense the change in the weather, running crazily round and round the lawn. Amy called her several times, as the men brought in the furniture that had been out of doors all summer. There was an air of expectancy in the air. But though the thunder grumbled away behind the crags, nothing happened until the dead of night.

Amy woke at about six. It was light, and there was something different. In a second she realised—the beck was flowing again. Its musical trickle gave her spirits a boost—at least there would not be a drought this year. But they had been perilously close. Arthur and Ruth Taylor trundled three large barrels outside to catch the still falling drizzle—just in case. But the sky was leaden grey. There was no way this was only a shower. They were back to typical Lakeland weather with a splash!

Amy put on her wellingtons to cross the meadow that Monday morning. They were her regular wear, and her voluminous cape and hood kept both her body and her newspapers dry. Nell splashed in the wet grass, her open mouth looking like a grin of delight. 'Well, lass, back to normal, eh?'

'Yes, Mr Gately. Just in time?'

'Just in time, if you ask me.'

'Except for the September campers. They'll have got a soaking.'

'Campers are used to it. Part of fun.' Mr Gately grinned. 'I reckon it's nearly Christmas now—I've already ordered my Christmas cards and wrapping paper. Is that young man of yours coming up for the holiday?'

'If you mean Dr Mac junior, I doubt it very much, Mr Gately.' Amy's voice went superior. 'He's not one of us, like his father was. He'll be living it up in the ritzy hotels, if I know anything about him.'

The Major was already downstairs when Amy arrived back for breakfast. 'Couldn't find a comfortable spot,' he explained. 'Sorry to be a nuisance. I know the rain is welcome, but it seems to have found my rusty hip all right.'

Amy shook her cape outside. 'I'll get on to the hospital this minute.' She rang the orthopaedic department as soon as the clock showed nine. The Major was prepared to pay for his operation, but she knew that he was not as well off as some of the others, and the two thousand pounds would leave very little of his private savings. He would only have his pension then. 'Hello? Is that the orthopaedic secretary?'

A deep masculine voice answered, rich and what Amy called fruity. 'Hello?'

'This is Amy Taggart, Greyrigg Manor old people's home. Is that Mr Kay's secretary?'

'You're speaking to Mr Kay, Amy. My secretary's gone on an errand for me. What can I do for you?'

The voice sounded kind, unhurried. She could imagine him leafing casually through the morning's mail on his secretary's desk. She said, 'About Major Hendon —Charles Hendon. He's on your list for a total hip.'

'He is indeed. I recall the gentleman. He was wondering how long he had to wait?'

'He was, sir.'

'Now hang on, Amy. I've got the paperwork right here.' She heard him opening and closing a couple of drawers. 'It looks as though he's got a wait of three or four months. Is there a problem?'

'Well, yes. He's a brave man, but he can scarcely sit down any more. May I send him along for another X-ray?'

A hearty and authoritative laugh. 'Never mind the X-ray. If he's that bad send him along next Thursday.'

'Thursday?' Amy had to repeat it, to make sure she heard aright.

'The woman who was due then isn't too bad. I saw her recently, and her pain is bearable. Let's do the Major first, shall we? He deserves it, the old warhorse.'

'That's extremely kind of you,' said Amy gratefully.

'Common sense. Get him to G3 on Thursday. We'll do the X-rays and tests then. If he's fit enough, by Monday night he'll be minus the bit that hurts.'

'You're very kind, Mr Kay.'

'Tell me, Amy, it was your place where Dr Mac lived, wasn't it?'

'Yes. He died in June.'

'I was wondering—does he have a son? Christopher, a physician?'

'Yes, he's in Harley Street. He owns the Manor now.'

'Good lord! We were at medical school together. Ask him to look me up next time he comes up, would you? Paul Kay. My number isn't in the book, so take it now, there's a good girl.'

She wrote it down. 'I'm very grateful to you,' she said.

'I'll look forward to meeting your Major again.'

Amy took Major Hendon in as requested. He was in so much pain that a major operation didn't bother him. 'Glad to get it over,' he said, as she helped him settle in bed, and chatted to the Sister on the ward.

It was drizzling when she got back. It drizzled for a fortnight. But after the beauty of the summer, Amy didn't mind. It was still grand and spectacular. And some of the leaves were beginning to turn gold and red and russet. She walked up the drive with a relief that another problem was being solved. Life was a succession of challenges. With a family of eighteen, plus the staff, there was scarcely a day without someone having a problem. As she went inside and shook back her damp hair, it was Quintin this time.

'My love, I don't think much of that rough young man who's come to look at the barn roof,' he told her.

'Jack Penny? He's a treasure. Knows everything there is to know about roofs.'

'Are you absolutely sure?'

'Quintin, what's the trouble?' asked Amy.

'He was very rude about my drawings.'

'Oh, Quintin, don't let him worry you. He's a blunt man, but he does know his job. We have to get the repairs and the insulation done before we need to get your plans out.'

Quintin looked hurt. 'He has a very crude way of telling one things!' Amy hid a smile, and mollified him by promising to take him to the Pheasant for lunch. Ever since the first trip there, Quintin had had a healthy respect for Tom Bright's beer, and made a single pint last the length of his ploughman's lunch. They went in Amy's battered little estate car. The Jaguar had been housed in the barn, out of the rain and the building dust. Amy secretly hoped that Quintin would have left before they started work on the interior of the barn—housing the Jaguar would then become a problem.

They came back about three. Larry Ford was just leaving. And as Quintin's mood had been greatly cheered by the reverent glances from the regulars in the pub—he always assumed they were reverent—Amy left him to his own devices, and went to speak to Larry.

The young GP showed Amy the bunch of prescriptions he had written. 'Anything I've forgotten?' he asked.

'Did you examine Doris?'

'She looked bright as a button today.'

'You thought she might have a hiatus hernia?'

'Oh yes, her stomach pains—burning in character. Hiatus hernia is the most likely. Shall I take another look?'

'Please, Larry. The pain she had the other night was colicky, not burning. From the position in the right hypochondrium I thought of gallstones.'

'Well, let's take a look. We can always arrange tests. Now that they do the scan instead of those awful tests, it's over in a jiffy.'

As they came down the stairs again, after deciding that it was impossible to diagnose Doris's pain until she got it again, and could show them where it was, Larry wrote down that he must make a hospital appointment for a scan. 'And Amy, can you be frank with me?' he added.

'Yes, sure. What about?'

He scratched his nose with the end of his pen, then nervously smoothed back his lock of pale hair. 'I've asked Sharla to dinner—a couple of times now. Does she really have to work every evening? She always says she's too busy.'

'Sharla, eh? I see.'

'That is the most unhelpful comment you ever made!'

Amy smiled up at him. 'Oh, Larry, she doesn't mean to be standoffish. She likes you very much, she's said so. But she's had a bad few years. There's a divorce soon to be finalised. You must understand she's afraid she'll get hurt again. It will take time.'

'Do you think she might come with you?'

Amy smiled. 'Good idea. Let's take Quintin too—just an informal outing? That way I can chat to Quintin, and you and Sharla can get to know each other better.'

'You—don't mind—me mentioning it?'

Amy knew what was in his conscientious and considerate mind. 'Larry, I don't consider you my property,' she told him. He had taken her out pretty regularly in the past six years, and he was now excusing himself in the nicest possible way.

And so autumn progressed in traditional way, with many wet days, but with some of the most glorious days, when the sun bathed the golden trees with light, and all the amateur artists in the county came out with their easels and their paintboxes, and made their feeble human efforts to imitate God's splendour.

The first day of October was a Friday. Amy got up to the swishing of water, and knew there was a real downpour. She didn't really mind. Nor did Nell. Amy pulled on her wellington boots, and gave a cheerful whistle as she covered her head with the khaki cape hood, right down over her eyes. On the way along the road she pulled a hazel staff to help her keep her footing. They climbed carefully over the stile—the wood was slippery with so much rain.

On the way back she stopped in the very middle of the meadow to look around her. The entire landscape was screened by a beautiful greyish-yellow light, as the sun made efforts to pierce the cloud. There was no way to describe it. She just felt choked with happiness, that she was able to live among this kind of magic.

She stumped her staff in front of her, taking extra care across the stile because of the pile of newspapers. And she wondered if the Major was getting his *Times* in the hospital. His operation had been successful, but the wound was slow to heal.

It was only as she descended the stile to the road that she realised a car was parked just opposite the stile. It was a white car, long and sleek, and now that she saw it, she recalled hearing the sound of an expensive engine while she was in Mr Gately's.

She almost thought she recognised the car. Except that it was totally impossible for Chris MacFarlane to be in Daweswater village at eight o'clock on a Friday morning. Her heart gave an unexpected jump, like it used to when she woke up on Christmas mornings when she was a child, before Dad got ill . . . The driver had lowered his window as she approached. She brushed the rain from her eyes, and looked down into Chris's dear, strange but familiar face. 'Can I give you a lift anywhere?' He wasn't smiling, waiting for her to show if she were pleased to see him.

Nell barked and jumped up, putting wet paws on the car. Chris patted her. Amy said, 'I can't. I'm soaking, and your car is much too posh.'

'Get in, Amy.' He spoke with impatience. 'Why do you think I got here just at this time?'

She tried to shake herself, but he wouldn't have it, pulling her in and taking the pile of papers from her, throwing them in the back seat. 'There, that's better. You aren't too delighted to see me, then. Think I've come to snoop?'

If only you knew, she thought. Her heart was throb-

bing like thunder that she thought he would hear. Her
first thought was that she must look absolutely awful.
She stole a glance at him, then her eyes widened. He was
wearing an old sweater, jeans, and he was unshaven.
'Chris, are you all right?' she asked anxiously.

He smiled then. 'Fine. I was at a party, and I suddenly
felt very bored with the company. So I decided to come
here—where I'm never bored.'

'Quintin will be glad to see you.'

'How nice,' he said drily. He turned back to the wheel
and started the engine. They arrived at the door of
Greyrigg without another word. Amy sat for a while,
wishing she dared throw her arms round his neck. But
she felt too ugly and most unattractive.

'I ought to tidy myself up,' she said. 'But you'll have to
put up with me like this for a while, because I think you
need a decent breakfast first of all.'

She turned to face him. He also was still sitting
without moving. Their eyes met. She had almost forgotten the full force those keen eyes could have when they
were fixed on her with a certain amount of meaning. She
followed the beloved lines of his face, and almost without knowing it, she put her fingers to his cheek, and
rubbed gently at the stubble of a beard. Chris caught her
hand and held it there for a moment. 'I've brought a
razor,' he said, his voice sounding a little hoarse. 'But I'd
like to have breakfast with you, if you don't mind? I
enjoyed it last time. And you did promise to spoil me a
little next time I came to the Manor.'

She opened the car door, and got out, scrabbling for
the papers. Then she ran in, trying to stifle her elation.
'Gwyn, make mine breakfast for two. Chris is here.
We'll eat in the dining room.'

She pulled off her raincape and threw the stick into a
corner. She tried to compose her face as Chris followed
her in, after saying good morning to Gwyn. To her
amazement, his eyes showed a light that reflected her
own, as he sat down with a sigh of pleasure, and said,
'Isn't it a lovely morning?' The rain drenched down.

CHAPTER EIGHT

THEY breakfasted together; no one else was down at this hour. Hannah and Gerald had arrived, and were chatting in the kitchen with Gwyn. And as they ate the bacon and eggs, the toast and marmalade, they recalled that day on the boat in high summer. Amy was still surprised that he could be in such good humour, almost as though he had been looking forward to coming. 'I thought you would be too busy to pay us another visit before the winter holiday.'

'I'm supposed to be skiing at Christmas.'

'Ah, I see.' With Francesca, no doubt. 'Will Quintin be going?'

Chris laughed. 'Old Quint's a coward, he hates physical activity. But I expect he'll come if we're all going.' He put down his fork. 'Have you ever skied, Amy?'

'Oh yes. We usually do a little in January or February. But it isn't the same afterwards here.' She smiled. '*Après-ski* in Kilderton is a carton of chips with a plastic fork!'

Chris looked thoughtful as he picked up his knife and fork again. 'I wonder how Four Winds is doing? I know I'm still paying the neighbour to keep an eye on the place. Maybe I'll have time to take a look today.'

'You ought to rest. There's a spare bed in Quintin's room.'

'Maybe I will. But I'm hoping to sit in on a meeting of you three wise men today, so if you start one, will you wake me up?'

Friday was a quiet day. Arthur and Ruth usually went to the market for fresh fruit and vegetables that they didn't have in the garden. Today Sharla and Quintin were to join Amy in the barn, to inspect Jack Penny's work, and see what needed doing next. Amy excused

herself to comb her hair and make herself presentable
before doing a quick check on all her guests, stopping for
a chat, and making sure everyone was all right.

Edna Bell was improving. And each time she had a
further success, an increase of power in the leg, another
ounce of strength in her fingers, her optimism grew.
'Maybe Graham will bring you along to the barn,' said
Amy. 'As soon as the place is warm and dry, we can start
taking the beds in, and that will free another room in the
main building—in case we're asked to take in another
three or four patients from Heaton Grange.'

The rain was still sheeting down. Amy looked out of
the window at Chris's car getting wetter and wetter, and
tried to convince herself he was really here. What urged
him to drive through the night, to come up to this
out-of-the way place? She decided he must distrust them
to run Greyrigg properly, and had come to keep an eye
on her. It was annoying, really. Yet she couldn't help the
feeling of elation at seeing him again, the strange rush of
adrenalin to her body in his vital presence.

She heard Quintin go downstairs, and his cry of
delight at seeing his friend. There was a lot of animated
conversation, then they came up again—Quintin must
be showing him where the spare towels were, and which
bed was his to rest on. She didn't intend to listen, but her
door was ajar, and they were next door. 'So Fran wants
to go to Biarritz?'

Chris's voice was less clear. 'Nothing's arranged. I'm
not sure if I have the time.'

'Come on, old boy, you always say you need your
holidays to unwind from the job. Don't tell me you've
changed.'

'Look, you go with Sonia. She's been ringing for you,
you know. You've made it clear that she isn't the light of
your life.'

'Nonsense. But I want to do some good here, Chris. I
know you've given that woman a free hand—not a wise
move in my opinion. But I love this place. I want to be
here to see some of my ideas to fruition.'

That woman. So that was what they thought of Amy Taggart! Amy closed her door silently and ran downstairs, her feet making no sound in her casual shoes. She didn't want to be talked about, least of all by Chris. She already knew he saw her as a disruptive nuisance. It stung her even more to be 'that woman'. She put on her thick woollen cardigan over her jeans and checked shirt, and ran across to the barn. Only Jack Penny and his young lad were in there, working already. She looked up in delight. 'I say, Jack, you've been working fast. It already looks like a palace!'

He grinned and waved. 'Ah knew rain was comin'. You don't want place damp, so we did slates first. It's okay now if you want to get central heatin' folk in. Walls be solid, and floor's pretty good too.'

'That's great.' She looked up, where Jack had fixed a false ceiling, to keep the place warmer, and to put concealed lighting. To Amy's eyes it was better than Quintin's scheme—more suited to the stone construction. She waved to Jack and walked to the other end of the barn. The rain drummed on the roof. She went into the small room at the end, where originally the farmer had his office. There was no furniture, but a couple of planks of wood. Amy sat down and put her chin in her hands.

She was pleased with the way the work was going, but disturbed at Chris's being there. It irritated her and upset her usual calmness and capability. Perhaps he had gone for a sleep. She hoped so, because Sharla and Quintin would be coming to see the work, and she would feel inhibited if Chris came too.

She forgot to think, gazing ahead and listening to the eternal rain. She had heard it a million times before. Why did it seem so sad—just today? And she did not try to answer her own question, because she knew . . .

A deep voice, gentle: 'I wondered where you'd got to.'

Amy looked up, bringing herself back to reality. He had shaved, and looked alert and, of course, dashingly handsome. His hair curled round his ears and over his forehead. It needed cutting really, if he wanted to look businesslike for his patients, but it looked right with his jeans and sweater. She loved him very much at that moment, and it interfered with her ability to make casual conversation. 'Here I am.'

He came and sat beside her on the planks. 'You look sad. If all this is getting on top of you, I won't be a brute and say I told you so.'

'It isn't,' she snapped. 'I came over to talk to Jack Penny. I wish you and Quintin would stop wanting me to give in! I'm enjoying the work—and I think Jack's made a marvellous job of the roof.'

'So do I.' He looked down at her, his blue eyes deep and sincere. 'Sorry.'

They sat for a while saying nothing. Amy had often wondered why he sought out her company and then sat silent. But she was getting used to him now, and did not expect conversation. She stole a sideways glance at him. He hadn't shaved very well—had he been in a hurry? And his eyes when you were close to him, looked tired and sad. Amy said, 'Come on, get it over. Tell me what I'm doing wrong—be honest! I know you have to do what Quintin and Francesca want. It's no secret. Don't let things rankle. I can take it now.'

Instead of the tirade she expected, Chris said quietly, 'I don't know what I want any more.'

Amy allowed her irritation to show. 'Then why on earth come all this way in all this weather? We were getting on very well without you. I did make you that promise. And I've asked Faith Hindle to come to the meeting this morning to take notes, so I could send you an account of what was decided.'

He was still quiet, unruffled by her straight talk. 'I didn't come to interfere. I thought I might be of help.' He turned to face her, and she met his blue gaze. 'Can't you get that into your head, Taggart? I want to help.'

'You could have helped so much better by leaving Quintin in London,' she told him.

'He was just so interested in the place. I had to bring him with me. He'd met Dad as well, and said he wanted to pay his last respects.'

'And you didn't want to annoy Francesca.'

He began to look annoyed then, but she didn't care any more. 'Don't be silly!' She said nothing, and after a while he said, 'It wasn't Francesca that made me friendly with him at school, you know. I was secretary of the rowing club, and he was just the right size to be cox. No one would take the job, because it always meant being chucked in the water after a race. I was given the job of being nice to Quint. It was a bit of joke at first, because he hated sports—all sports, and nobody thought I'd succeed. I did get him—and in the process, I realised that he was a nice harmless little guy, and I started to look after him a bit.'

'And the lovely Francesca had nothing at all to do with it.'

Chris forced her to look at him again. His lips showed the hint of a smile as he said, 'You look nice when you're jealous.'

'Jealous? What utter rubbish!'

'Yes, isn't it? I met the girl when I went to Quint's place one weekend. He lives at Henley, so it wasn't far. We went there one half term—Dad was too busy for me to go home.' He was quiet again, and Amy felt sad for the schoolboy who wasn't wanted at home. 'Mum had died, and I didn't get on with Veronica. I used to go sometimes, naturally, but I never stayed long. I never felt comfortable at Four Winds after that. She made me feel like a stranger in my own house . . .'

'Dr Mac couldn't be unwelcoming,' protested Amy.

'No, on the contrary. He was great. But in his hurry to get me to med school, and to make sure I applied for the plum jobs and passed my Membership exams—well, our conversations usually consisted of nothing else.'

Amy said in a low voice, 'I'm beginning to understand.'

Chris said harshly, 'How I fell in love with Francesca?'

'No, not that. But Quintin's family—they were probably closer to you than your own father at that time . . . And Dr Mac—all his parental feelings were going to care for his patients. He did that so very well. They always came first with him. I thought it was good. Now I think it's a bit sad, really.'

'I'm not fishing for sympathy, Amy, only explaining how things happened for me. Quint's family were fun. They had some horses and a couple of boats.' He fell silent, as though thinking back to his schooldays, then he gave a huge yawn. 'I say, sorry, but I am hellishly tired.'

'You shouldn't have come. Why don't you go and lie down?'

'Trying to get rid of me?'

Amy's lip trembled suddenly, when she was not expecting it, and she blushed and turned away, so that she didn't see the look in his eyes. How could he ever believe that she would have sat there with him for the rest of her life, and never wanted to be rid of him? She felt his hand lightly round her shoulders, and gritted her teeth together so that she did not give way. He must have felt her body tensing at his touch, for he said very softly, 'Hey, Amy, look at me!'

She fumbled in her sleeve for a handkerchief—she could pretend to blow her nose or something. At that moment there were footsteps outside the barn. Olive Park was running in, a raincoat over her head. 'Amy, the ambulance can't come for Doris, for her gall-bladder scan. There's been a pile-up on the motorway, and there are no free ambulances.'

'How is she feeling?' Amy stood up, her voice again under her own control. 'I'll go and have a word.'

Chris followed, and Amy explained what Doris's trouble was. 'Let me take a look at her,' he said. 'I've got my instruments in the car.'

Doris was in her room, looking wan. She had been dressed to go to the hospital, and now she took off her coat, and sat, breathing rather heavily, in her armchair. Chris came forward, with a professional smile. 'My hands are clean, Doris. Can I just take a look at your tummy?' She lay on the bed, and Chris examined her with great care and detail. He listened to her chest, checked her blood pressure twice, and pressed various areas of her plump abdomen with skilled fingers. Amy looked away. His hands were so attractive—and the last thing a Sister should be thinking about was what other things those fingers could do . . .

Then Doris gave a little squeak of pain. 'There's no doubt, Doris, it is a stone. And you aren't too fit for a general anaesthetic, with that chest of yours. So what I'll do is prescribe something for the pain. And then we'll prescribe something that will melt the stone away, without need of surgery.' Chris made some notes on a small pad.

The little ex-schoolmistress said, 'That sounds a bit like magic.'

He grinned as she buttoned up her dress. 'In a way it is, I suppose. I think you're supposed to close your eyes and say you believe in fairies.'

She laughed. 'I used to get my class to do that when we read *Peter Pan*. I'm afraid children these days just give a raucous laugh at the new meaning of the word!'

Chris finished writing. 'They're wrong. There's still magic around, Doris, if you know where to look. Now I'll see how quickly we can start this treatment for you, just as soon as I've had a word with Dr Ford. It wouldn't be ethical for me to treat you without his permission.'

Her friend Martha Quayle came to the door, and was delighted in the change in her. She hobbled over to sit with Doris, and the two ladies sat with much relief, chatting together. Amy heard something of their conversation—all praise for Chris's kindness, and his skill . . .

'He's like his father, you know. When he gets older, you'll see.'

When Amy went downstairs Chris had disappeared. Perhaps he was at last taking that nap, after phoning Larry about Doris's gallstone. Amy went on towards the barn, where Faith Hindle was waiting with her notebook and pen, chatting coquettishly with Jack Penny, who had stopped work for a brew-up. 'Yes, Dr Mac is back again. He's a lovely fellow. Does us good just to see him walking around like someone out of *Dynasty*!'

Jack listened sagely. 'You want to watch them handsome ones. Break yer 'eart, they would. You need a nice steady chap, not a pretty boy.'

'Huh, you're telling me who I want? I'd just like to sample his bedside manner, I tell you. I'd make him —Oh, hello, Amy!'

Amy couldn't help smiling. 'Your conversation is very predictable, Faith. Have you got your notebook?'

'Yes, and my knitting, in case it gets boring.'

'I don't think we'll need notes taking, since Dr MacFarlane is here in the flesh.'

'And what flesh! I wouldn't mind a bit . . .'

'Faith, please don't be tiresome.' But Amy was annoyed at herself as well as Faith, knowing she felt the same in Chris's presence.

Edna and Graham Bell appeared at the door of the Manor, and Amy went across to bring Graham and the wheelchair under one large umbrella. 'Sharla won't be long,' she told him. 'You aren't too cold?'

'No, in spite of the rain, it isn't too chill today.' Graham wheeled his wife to a central place in the barn. There were some small baskets of equipment by the wall, and he handed her a rubber ball to squeeze.

There seemed to be a lot of traffic on the road outside. Amy looked out of the window to see what was rumbling so loudly. A huge pantechnicon was backing up the drive towards the front portico. She went dashing out, forgetting to cover herself against the rain. 'I say, are you sure you have the correct address, lads?' she called.

'There ain't another Greyrigg Manor in these parts, I 'ope?'

'No.'

The driver jumped out. 'Sign 'ere, love.' Amy took the paper. It read 'Patterton's Medical and Surgical

Supplies.' Underneath was a list of all the equipment that Sharla had listed when Amy had asked her to forget about money. It was all there. Her eyes were large, as the two men started unloading the van. She pointed to the barn, and the items were carried in one by one, Amy standing in the rain, watching like a child on Christmas Day.

'Like it?'

She turned. Chris was standing there with Sharla, whose expression matched Amy's. Amy said inadequately, 'It's lovely.'

'Useful too.'

'Yes.'

'Just a little gift.'

She nodded. A basketball fell from one of the parcels and Sharla picked it up with delight. Amy said ironically, 'Our own basketball team too.'

Chris said, 'Ball work helps balance, so Sharla tells me. And the Major will enjoy basketball—he told me he was a champion in his young days.'

Mention of the Major reminded her of Mr Kay. 'I say, Chris, can I have a word with you?' she asked. They left Sharla having a session with the Bells, and all of them having a good look at all the new equipment. They went back to the Manor, and Amy explained about Mr Kay, producing his phone number.

'Paul Kay? Wonderful! We cut up our first body together! He was hopeless. You see what surgical training can do?'

'Don't forget to ring,' Amy reminded him. 'He was so helpful to us, taking Major Hendon so promptly.'

'That sounds like Professor Jackland's training. He never allowed us to forget to treat each patient as a human being first, with a life of his own and a family. The disease came second. I always remember one of our group referring to "the cirrhosis in bed twelve". He got a telling off we've all never forgotten!'

When Chris was relaxed, he lost the lines round his eyes, and the look of sadness. His face took on an

animation and an animal attraction that Amy felt she
could gaze at all day. But when he looked at her and
caught her staring, she was afraid again, nervous in case
he could read her mind, the way she had imagined he
could when they had first met by his father's grave.

He smiled. He was sitting at her desk in the office,
where they had gone to find the phone number. She was
perched on the desk, where she could see the hall and
the open door. The rain had stopped, and there was a
gleam of sun catching the polished mahogany of the big
sideboard. 'Well, you got what you wanted, my little
nagging friend,' remarked Chris.

She replied sharply, 'I don't nag for myself. But I'll do
anything for my family.'

'I know.' His voice was suddenly warm. 'You'd do
anything for your patients. How old were you when you
lost your father?'

'Sixteen.' She thought back to that sad time. It was
quite obvious that she had adopted all her old people to
fill the gap in her heart. And Chris understood. 'I don't
think I said thank you for all the equipment,' she told
him.

'No need. There's more to come. I want to make the
small room into an indoor heated pool. Am I allowed?'

'Chris, this is costing a fortune already! You're the
one who gave me such a lesson in economics! How can
you afford all this?'

'Tell you one day,' he grinned.

'In that case, I think you ought to apologise to me for
the telling off. You've been much more extravagant than
I would ever be.'

'I'll apologise if you'll take me sailing.'

'Now?'

'It's stopped raining.'

'I know that, but . . . Oh, all right, let's go.'

With a nervous energy generated by his presence,
Amy grabbed her anorak and began to run down the
drive. She had crossed the road, gone through the
kissing gate, and was almost at the jetty when Chris

caught her up. They were both laughing, and her heart was crying, that they could have such fun, and yet know it was only for a very short time. They strolled more gently the last few yards to the jetty. *Speedwell* was none too clean, and Chris set to with willingness, wiping the timbers down and shaking out the sail. They worked feverishly, as though it was better than having to talk. When he finally pushed the boat out and moored her properly to the jetty, he said, 'I hope you didn't have anything else to do. I was being selfish, dragging you away.'

'I felt like it too.' She was still a little breathless from the exertion.

'You don't usually sail on a Friday afternoon.'

'Not usually.'

He took the tiller, without her permission, and hoisted the sail. There was quite a fresh wind today, and there wasn't much conversation, as they sped along, as usual feeling free and relaxed away from the normal tensions of everyday life. Chris said, raising his voice in the wind, 'Somehow I feel I've only got to know my father since knowing you. I'm glad I met you.'

Amy didn't reply, looking down earnestly at a shoal of sticklebacks, under the bows. The wind slackened a little, and the quiet of the lake and the majestic fells all around them made them feel small and vulnerable. She met Chris's look. 'Are you?' She didn't know what else to say.

'You made me think a lot—what kind of man I am, what I really want from life. And it was strange, coming up against a different view of Dad. I thought he'd not been fond of me, but here he seems to be looked on as a saint.'

'He was just a man,' said Amy. 'No one expects anyone to be perfect.'

He smiled then. 'So why did you nag me? I'm not perfect.'

She was stung into an answer. 'I thought we'd finished that joke. If you don't stop telling me what a nuisance I

am to you, I'll just have to cry, because as far as I can see,
it's the only weapon I have left.'

Chris pulled on the sheet. 'Let's go back, we might
miss lunch.'

'It's only cottage pie. You'd get a better meal at the
Meridien. It's your type of place.'

It was Chris's turn to snap. 'I wish you'd stop
pigeonholing me! I know what type of place I like! And I
adore cottage pie.'

'If I'd known you were going to shout at me so much,
I would have let you come out alone. It isn't much
fun——' Amy broke off abruptly, as Farmer Crabtree's
son came chugging out in his tiny motorboat, his fishing
line at the ready. He waved to her, and positioned
himself in his favourite bay, before cutting the engine.
Amy and Chris both realised how sound travels over
water. The middle of Daweswater was not the ideal
place for a quarrel—not unless they wanted all the
farmsteads along the shoreline to know their arguments.
They sailed back to the jetty in total silence. But as they
came alongside and Amy jumped out to moor the boat,
she caught Chris's eye, and they both burst out laughing.
'I'm sorry, Amy, for not being perfect. I'll have to try
harder.'

'Don't bother. I'm pretty imperfect myself.'

They took care to leave the little boat tidy. Then they
set off up the meadow, their feet squelching a bit in the
wet grass. 'Well, thanks for the sail,' said Chris. 'I
don't often spend Fridays on a lake.'

'What would you be doing today normally?' Amy
asked.

'Just patients in the morning, and visits in the afternoon. Someone would probably ring and tell me where
the party was tonight. But I don't always go these
days—must be getting old.'

'Or maybe it's what you said—about getting to know
yourself. I believe people who want to be busy, or to be
with people all the time, probably dare not face themselves. They possibly don't even know who they are.

Maybe they don't want to know.'

'So you think I'm growing up at last, Amy Taggart?'

She adored the way he said her name. It used to annoy her, but now she loved him to say it like that. 'I'm no authority on you,' she told him.

'You know more about me than anyone else.'

'I do?'

'Yes.' And he put one hand gently on her shoulder as they walked together up to the kissing gate. She tensed at once, knowing that it meant nothing to him. He would arouse her to a state of longing, and then drive back in his BMW to his parties and his girls. Off in a puff of smoke . . . Chris said gently, 'Is this what's called a kissing gate?'

'Yes.'

'How does it work?'

'Never mind.' Electrified by his closeness, she tried to squeeze through without opening it properly, but Chris held the swinging gate so that she was trapped in the V of the fence. Then he bent and kissed her lips, cool in the wind, coolly and sweetly and hungrily.

Neither of them spoke until they got inside the Manor again. Amy's heart was beating painfully, too painfully even for her to tell him off in fun. No words would come, except the ones she dared not say—I love you with all my heart . . . The touch of his kiss was still on her lips, meaning so much to her, and so little to him.

It was fortunate that Aggie Brown was in the hall. She was on her way to the office to see Amy, and beamed when she saw her coming in. 'I want to put my name down for church, Amy love. I missed because of the food poisoning, and then I didn't go because it wasn't Canon Forrester.'

'Okay, Aggie, I'll put you down. We will have the mini-bus on Sunday. Arthur's doing a service on it this afternoon.' Life was going on as usual. Only it wasn't usual for Amy, and she wanted to run away, except there was no place to run to. And Chris stayed with her. 'Why don't you go for lunch?' she asked him.

He said, 'We'll go together. It's easier for Gwyn.'

The dining room was emptying. Ruth saw them coming, and brought them their cottage pie, kept warm for them. 'You been sailing on a day like this?' she asked.

Chris explained, 'I have to sail when I can, whatever the weather.'

'Well, I can't say I'd enjoy it.'

'*We* did,' said Chris. And Amy stuck her fork in her potato, and kept her face down.

'Amy?'

They had eaten as much as they could. She looked up, facing him at last. He said, 'Why am I always saying sorry to you? Isn't there anything I do that pleases you, woman? Come on, now, please don't look so appalled! It was only a kiss.'

She swallowed the lump in her throat. He was right; she was being unnecessarily touchy. She managed a tight-lipped smile. 'I was miles away. What did you say?'

'You heard.' His face was close to hers, and she ached with the need to be in his embrace. 'Didn't you?'

She tossed her head back. 'It's time we got down to work. Quintin will be waiting for your verdict on his plans. Shall we go to the barn?'

'Start without me. I'll be along shortly.' He touched her hair as he went past her chair.

CHAPTER NINE

AMY stopped to chat to Arthur, who had brought the mini-bus round to the covered yard, and was just checking the tyre pressures. The Manor was going on in its usual way, with Ruth in the garden, Gwyn in the kitchen, most of the guests now going to their rooms for a nap, and Nell 'helping' Mary with the window-cleaning. Everything was normal—except for the white BMW parked in the drive, and the presence in their midst of a tall physician with whom the Manor had nothing in common whatsoever. He didn't belong here. Why had he come?

Sharla came running out, forgetting her coat in her excitement. 'Isn't it wonderful to have everything we want? And you see, the Urias splints will be useful for Edna! If we can't get her walking now, then I don't deserve to be allowed to stay.'

'Oh, don't say that, Sharla. You're part of the furniture now. We'd be lost without you.' Amy ran after her into the barn, where they surveyed the mass of helpful gadgets, strewn rather haphazardly around. 'Shall we try to find cupboards for this stuff?'

The two girls happily arranged the things, Sharla checking each one on the copy of the list the van driver had left with them. Everything they had wanted was there. Chris must have sent the entire list to Patterton's.

Amy went ahead with the tidying up. She welcomed Quintin when he finally turned up to criticise the improvements for himself. But he had to admit that the barn was beginning to look good. After what Chris had told her about Quintin, Amy found herself being nice to him. He hadn't had an easy schooling. Money wasn't everything. She began to feel grateful to Chris for not allowing Quintin to be thrown in the water.

There was no real need for discussion, because the next step was the central heating man. 'Just so as he remembers that we have an emergency generator, if the central supplies are cut off.'

Quintin agreed. 'It's frightfully primitive in some ways, this part of the world. But it has its good points —starting with Tom Bright's beer!'

Amy laughed. 'You're almost a countryman now, Quintin. Only you'll have to go to London for your clothes. King's Road, isn't it?'

It was already getting late in the afternoon. The sun had not stayed out, but the drizzle wasn't too serious. Amy and Sharla were drawn back to the Manor by the smell of freshly baked bread, but Quintin wanted to stay on, wandering round the barn, pretending that the false ceiling had been his idea. They left him to it. Jack Penny and his boy were just brewing up for the last time that day. Let them get together with Quintin, and he might learn a thing or two.

Over warm bread and farmhouse butter, Sharla spoke of the old days in London. Amy didn't interrupt. Maybe this was the time she would mention her daughter. 'We had such a nice crowd at St George's. But these things never last.'

'You've stayed friends with Chris.'

'Chris was special—so thoughtful. I used to wonder how he became successful in Harley Street, when he was so unwilling to take money from sick people.' Sharla laughed. 'Ray wasn't so high-principled. He was longing for private practice, but he was specialising in ENT and the rooms were overcrowded with surgeons willing to make their fortunes out of tonsils and adenoids.'

Amy encouraged her gently. 'Go on. It wasn't money that split you up.'

Sharla sighed. 'No. We both had good jobs. He just wasn't ready to be—well, a—father.' She looked with her black eyes apprehensive, to see what Amy would think. Amy waited. Sharla went on, 'I was so happy to be pregnant. I knew I could be a good mother. But when she—Shakira—was born—I lost my senses, Amy. I became very ill—disorientated and depressed. It was so awful, because she was a beautiful little thing.' Tears welled in her eyes. Amy longed to tell her that Chris was working even now to get Shakira back to her, but it would be wrong to say anything.

'Where is she now?' she asked.

'With a relative. I will have to prove that she has a stable home to go to before the courts will give her back to me.' The emotions that had been suppressed for so long burst out, and Sharla put both hands in front of her face. They were sitting in an alcove, unobserved by the others in the room.

Amy waited until her storm of weeping died down. She leaned forward as Sharla mopped her red eyes. 'Sharla, no one is saner than you. This is your home, if you want to stay. So there's no possible reason why we shouldn't get in touch with that relative of yours, and let her know that Greyrigg Manor will be getting ready to welcome its newest and youngest resident.'

Sharla sat back. 'You honestly think I'm cured?'

'I never thought there was anything wrong,' said Amy. 'Naturally I've seen you weeping in secret, but anyone would weep, who had a child she hadn't seen for three months. I'm amazed you have carried on so bravely for so long.'

'You like babies, Amy?'

'I adore babies, but I have to confess I'm not very experienced with them. Oh, Sharla, wouldn't it be perfect if she could be here for Christmas? I—I'm sure she's a beautiful girl. When is her birthday?'

'April the ninth.'

Amy was deeply touched. To give up a baby at two or three months must be one of the hardest things to do. Sharla had been through a tough time. Maybe it would take longer than she thought for Larry Ford to be able to heal some of the hurts she had suffered. But at least it was hopeful that the young doctor was taking an interest. They would be so good for each other. But it wasn't her business, and she knew she could only be encouraging and as helpful as she could. 'I'm sure Chris will get things moving for us,' she said. 'We'll have a word with him before he goes home.'

Quintin joined them then, and their talk turned to the barn, or as he now named it, the physiotherapy wing. The girls were amused, but proud at the same time. 'And Jack Penny did it well, Quintin. Stage one is over now. Only the central heating and a coat of paint.'

He looked slightly disgruntled. 'According to my suggestions, there ought to be three sections. And I did sketch in larger windows. I feel the scale of the building needs longer, more graceful window frames, don't you, Amy?'

'I see your point, Quintin, but it's a workroom, not a mansion.' She tried not to gloat, not to make it obvious that she was in charge, that the tables had been turned on young Quintin. For all his fancy ways, she had begun to realise, as Chris had done, that he wasn't so bad, and she quite liked him now.

Chris didn't turn up for the discussion; perhaps he had at last gone to catch up on his sleep. Amy wasn't sorry. He was far too disturbing an influence, and she found things went much more smoothly without him.

That evening, after most of the guests had been seen to bed, she sat with Sharla in the lounge. 'I'm glad we've got all your problems sorted out,' she said.

'So am I. It's a tremendous relief. I wish I'd told you earlier, but I was ashamed of my own silliness. It was wrong—I should put Shakira's happiness first.'

'And ours. Can you just see the look of delight on Aggie Brown's face when she sees her? Or Peggy Bickerstaffe, Doris or Martha? It will do more good than your ballroom dancing, I can tell you.'

'Oh, come on, Amy!' Sharla was completely relaxed now, her face showing more animation then ever before. 'You're going to be proud of our dancers, I promise you. They'll love it.'

'Well, I suppose it can't do any harm,' shrugged Amy.

Just then Chris and Quintin came in together. From Quintin's talkative manner, it was clear they had been to the Pheasant. They came over to join the girls, Quintin doing most of the chatting, Chris sitting a little back, his handsome face in shadow. After a while he started talking to Sharla, and judging from the girl's face, about Shakira, and future plans for caring for her at the Manor. Chris was a good friend to have—kind and thoughtful and not a bit like the rest of his rich and sophisticated crowd. Yet he was quite happy to stay in that sort of life, apparently for ever. Once a city man, always a city man.

Amy was first to feel sleepy, and excuse herself. She was just tidying the office and putting off the light there, when Chris caught up with her, his step quiet in training shoes. 'Amy, Paul and Sylvia Kay have invited you to lunch tomorrow. I'm driving over to Galthwaite. You will come, won't you?'

'Couldn't you take Sharla?' she asked.

His face showed a flash of exasperation. 'They didn't invite Sharla! They invited *you*. Paul said you sounded like a really nice person. I didn't tell him you couldn't stand the sight of me. I thought you'd like to meet the great Mr Kay in person—it might be helpful next time you want an emergency admission! If you're on first name terms with the Chief, it always helps.'

'Okay. Thanks. It's all right to go to church first?'

'Do you have to?'

Prickled, Amy retorted, 'No, I don't have to. But I'd like to.'

'All right, we'll go straight on after church. We'll take my car. You don't have to drive the mini-bus, do you?'

'I can ask Arthur.' He turned away, and she called after him, 'Don't let me force you to come—I know you aren't a churchgoer. You can pick me up after the service.'

He was equally prickly. 'I'm not an atheist, you know. I'll be there.'

Amy was up at her usual early hour. The day was misty, autumnal in its dank but gentle start, promising a golden day. She and Nell had their usual gallop across a very dewy field, and her face was tingling with health when she got back with the Sunday papers. The sun was already warmer, as its rays pierced the mist in a spectacular way across the valley, hitting patches of golden bracken and purple heather.

When Amy came out of the portico in her best fawn suit, Chris was already in the car. But Aggie Brown was refusing to get into the mini-bus, protesting that nobody had brought her opening medicine. Amy looked down at Chris, who had opened the window to listen. The bus was in front of his car, so he couldn't start until Arthur moved. He cocked an eyebrow at Amy. 'What do we do now?' he wanted to know.

She smiled in recollection. 'Dr Mac always appealed to her better nature. But she doesn't have one if I try.'

'Want me to have a go?'

'Please. Miracles could happen.'

'Thank you for that total trust in my ability!' laughed Chris. 'I know Dad isn't me, and I'm not a patch on Dad—but I think I know how to handle this.' He was getting out of the car as he spoke, and he went over to Aggie, who stood firmly on her two little stumpy legs, refusing to be helped up the ramp. He bent and said a few quiet words to her. Amy watched the old face brighten, wrinkled but still attractive under the brown felt hat with a pheasant's feather. Then Aggie nodded, and allowed Chris to take her by the arm and walk into the bus with her. Chris came back with eyes downcast, and got back into the BMW.

Only when they were driving along the short stretch of road towards the village did he turn and give Amy a triumphant look. She had to smile. 'My turn to say sorry,' she told him.

'It's all right. You've no idea how much of an achievement I think it is. She's a stubborn old lady, there's no denying. But women are all alike basically. They respond to a little soft talking.'

'I must remember that,' Amy said wryly.

'I didn't mean you, of course. You don't respond at all.' Chris turned back to the wheel.

'I suppose it depends who does the talking,' she said sweetly, looking out of the window on her own side, as though Mrs Benson's garden wall was the most fascinating sight.

'And to think I could have stayed behind and read the *Sunday Times*!'

'Oh no, you couldn't. Quintin grabs that first.'

He sighed, as though realising that she wasn't going to let him have the last word. He drew up off the road on a patch of grass close to the church. 'Shall we go?'

Canon Forrester was pleased to see Chris at the simple little service, and shook hands with him heartily, saying it was good to have a Dr Mac in his congregation again. After they had said a goodbye, Amy paused, and without a word being spoken, both she and Chris turned and walked quietly to the little grave with its simple slate headstone. Roderick MacFarlane, beloved physician, passed away . . . the grave reminded Amy of the first time she had set eyes on Christopher, son of Roderick, tall, square-jawed, keen-eyed and totally sure of himself. She looked at him now. Those keen eyes were looking down at a beautiful arrangement of roses and ferns. 'Who put the flowers there, Amy?' he asked.

'Different people. The grave is always tended. Everyone in the village helps. Sometimes there are three or four posies on it.'

He seemed slightly uncomfortable. He bit his lip, and murmured in a gruff voice, 'That's nice of them.' And as they walked back to the car, he said, 'I think I'm getting to know Dad better now. You learn about people by the way they're remembered.'

Arthur Taylor came up to them. 'Aggie's missing again,' he announced.

Amy turned to Chris. 'It seems she wants a bit more of

your masculine charm. I know where she is.' And she
went back into the church, where the organist was just
putting his music away. Aggie was sitting in the front
pew, her eyes piously turned up towards heaven, her
hands together in a saintly pose.

Amy hid a smile, and went up to the little woman.
'Amen,' she whispered. Then she held out a hand, and
Aggie took it graciously. When they reached the bus,
Amy bent and kissed the wrinkled cheek. 'You're a
wicked old lady, always wanting attention,' she
whispered, and Aggie turned and cackled away, pleased
and proud of her own exploit.

The bus set off round the bend. Amy and Chris stood
together until it was out of sight. When she turned, she
saw that his eyes had been on her. There was something
in them she could not read, but it disturbed her. 'Shall
we go?' she said.

He seemed to pull himself together. 'Right.' There
was no aggression there, no wish to argue with her, none
of the acrimony that he was capable of putting into his
comments to her. They set off towards Galthwaite. By
now the mist had gone, and it was a glorious autumn day,
the trees all around them rampant in their late beauty,
especially the spreading beeches along the way,
shedding a perfect golden light on the place beneath.

There was no conversation on the way. Amy was
used to that—and she liked it, because what was in her
heart she could not say. She pointed out directions.
Galthwaite was only fifteen miles away.

Paul Kay was at the elegant gate of his magnificent
cottage to greet them. He was not tall, but he had a
presence, an aura of kindliness and humanity. He had a
mop of curly red hair, which he explained later was
inherited from his Irish grandfather. He opened his arms
when he saw them. 'Chris, my boy, you've worn well,' he
grinned.

'I've no choice, Paul. I've no one to spoil me. I live on
gruel.'

'With the occasional Veuve Clicquot, I've no doubt.

Harley Street does that to people.' Paul Kay turned to Amy. 'I did want to meet you. Your appealing little voice on the telephone talked so much sense.' He shook her heartily by the hand. 'Moved my stony heart, it did!'

They were ushered into a stone-flagged cottage, with Indian rugs of amazing luxury around the floors, and with enough archways to delight Quintin for a month. Sylvia came out of the kitchen when she heard voices. She was bubbly and charming, and very round, in the final stages of pregnancy. Chris was very complimentary. 'To think I could have lived like this if I'd joined my father!' he smiled.

'I don't regret it. But then I was never a city slicker like you.'

'And when the family comes along, won't you be glad!'

Paul was obviously proud of his child even before birth. 'I've decided to put him down for Manchester Grammar.' He gestured towards the extensive garden. 'The swing's going on that elm tree. And the cricket stumps against that wall.'

'Even if *she* doesn't like cricket.' Sylvia had come in with a tray of drinks. They stood around, and eventually took their drinks out into the garden. The sun was as warm as on a summer day, and the bees seemed galvanised into extra activity among the roses by the sudden heat. Sylvia had heard of Greyrigg, and its good reputation. 'We've had so many miscarriages that I thought I'd be putting Paul's name down for Greyrigg before we made it with a baby of our own.'

Amy decided that Sylvia was someone she would like to be friends with. And she confided that their physiotherapist was bringing her baby to live at Greyrigg. 'So you see, we have no age limits,' she told Sylvia.

Sylvia turned out to be an orthopaedic nurse, and she had many good ideas for the use of the equipment they had just acquired, promising to come along and see how it worked—and enthusiastic about the ballroom dancing.

'All right, woman, enough female gossip. I want my lunch!' Paul's sexist comments hid a gentle and loving soul, and Amy could take no offence at his jovial manner. Especially after the way he had taken the Major in so quickly. In fact, the four of them got on so well that they didn't notice how the time was passing.

On the way back, it was Amy who spoke first. 'You're sighing,' she told Chris.

'Am I? Maybe I don't feel like going back to London.'

'You've been very good to the Manor. Everyone's grateful.'

'I expect you thought that old Scrooge in Harley Street wouldn't do anything to help you. Well, now you know.'

She said after a pause, 'I'm sorry I nagged.'

'You're not. You enjoy nagging.'

'Do you really think so?'

He hadn't been driving very fast; these winding Lakeland roads were not made for speed. Chris drew in to a layby, and stopped the engine. 'Not really.' He turned towards her. 'I'll be leaving as soon as I've dropped you at Greyrigg. Do I get a thank-you kiss?'

Nervous, Amy leaned over and kissed his cheek. But it was like a drug that she wanted more of, and when he turned and took her in his arms, she made no protest. 'Happy Christmas, Amy.' So he wasn't coming, then. She put her arms around him, one hand behind his head, touching the curling hair on his neck. The sweetness was electrifying, as his kiss deepened. Yet it was all so brief, and he left her with a longing deeper than she could ever describe.

He didn't go at once, because Sharla wanted to talk about Shakira, while Quintin wanted to talk about Francesca and Sonia. Amy left the three friends to it, retiring tactfully to her own room. Let him go soon. The longer he stayed, the more she was tempted to go down and feast her eyes on him, remember every beautiful moment they had spent together.

She turned away from the window. There was no point in increasing her torture. She went and sat on her bed, yet hearing his voice through the open window, along with the bleating of the sheep, which sounded today particularly mournful and lonely. Tears filled her eyes. She knew he liked her; she knew that if she had shown she liked him, they would have had an affair. But she also knew that when it was over, there would be nothing else in her life. She would be devastated. She dared not accept his overtures, because she knew she would not survive the ending of it all.

At least now she could be strong enough to withstand him. Maybe in a few more years, she might meet someone who would be good to her, someone who might be able to fill the gaping cavity left by the one man she had ever loved. It wasn't the same with city people. Relationships meant so much less to them. They could love you today, forget you tomorrow. And that, Amy knew, would be the end of her. She couldn't live like that—and she wouldn't.

It seemed quiet outside. Chris must have gone. Amy went to her modest dressing-table, surveying the mess that was her face. She dabbed at the eyes, but nothing seemed to help the redness. She just had to go down. If she stayed here she would cry all night. She must and would go down, immerse herself in the problems and small troubles of her beloved family downstairs. She could forget herself with them. To them a tiny point like missing the post became an earth-shattering occasion.

She stood up, shook herself mentally, and pushed back her tangled curls. Right. They might make comments about her eyes, but she could say it was hay fever. She turned towards the door—then she gasped, and cried out in fear and longing. Chris stood there, his eyes dark with emotion. 'Amy, can we talk? Something's happening, and I can't go till we've talked it out.'

'I'd rather not.' She couldn't recall replying, but it was her voice that spoke.

'It's my life you're talking about! Don't treat it like some trivial nothing, like your patients. Please, Amy.'

'Your life and mine are very far apart, you know,' she reminded him.

'Do they have to be?'

She took a deep breath. Her heart was being wrenched out of her body, so great was the pain. But her common sense, stifled though it had been, forced the words from her mouth. 'Don't prolong it—don't! It makes no sense.' Doomed to failure—she knew she couldn't take that. Even today's anguish was preferable to that. She rushed past him, pulling her arm away as he caught it, feeling the touch like a scalding patch on her skin, as she hurried down and sat in a window seat with the Major, Frank Bates and Sarah-Jane Phelps.

And then Chris was at the door of the lounge. His eyes burned into her soul. She could not look away . . .

Major Hendon stood up, limping across to Chris on his crutches. 'We all thank you very much for what you've done for us,' he said. 'You've been so very kind.'

Chris took the outstretched hand. 'Think nothing of it. I wish you well—all of you.' And as he stood in the doorway, his eyes desperate, he was forced to shake hands with the guests who all had something to thank him for.

Gradually, Chris was swept back towards his car by a tide of people. Amy dared not stay behind, as it would stand out. She joined the back of the group. Chris was talking to Quintin now, shaking his hand once more. She heard him say, 'I didn't get to Four Winds this trip. I'd be grateful if you or Amy could call, make sure everything is all right there. The neighbour who's looking after it is Mrs Jolly. Let me know if you manage to get there.'

Quintin turned to look for Amy. 'You know where it is, Amy?' She nodded. 'Right, that's a promise, old man. Give my regards to the King's Road. And let me know about Biarritz.'

'Right, right.' Chris was in the BMW now, both windows wound right down. The warm sun blazed down on the garden. He put his hand out of the window to wave, and there was a chorus of goodbyes as the car backed slowly towards the road. Slowly, so slowly he went, looking behind one minute, and then back to wave the next. It was indeed a triumphal procession. But when he reached the road, he suddenly roared the engine, stamped on the accelerator, and zoomed from their sight like a rocket taking off. Amy listened to the tortured engine, being forced beyond what good driving should do. She heard him shoot into Daweswater village, slow up to cross the river, then turn up past the Meridien towards Kilderton. She heard the engine getting fainter and fainter. She heard the engine until way past bedtime, sitting at her window again, guessing where he had reached, praying that in his reckless hurry he would do nothing careless or wrong.

It was Sharla who came up, into the bedroom where she had not bothered to put the light on. 'Don't you want any supper, Amy? Are you all right?'

Amy knew she had to appear normal, or people would talk. 'I forgot—I was reading.' She pretended to put a magazine away, one that she had not in fact opened. Sunday evening supper was usually fish. She went down. Most of the plates were empty, as Gwyn brought her a generous portion of baked cod. It was delicious, as usual, but to Amy it might have been sawdust. She nibbled at it, trying not to attract notice by being off her food.

Sharla made things worse by talking of Chris. 'I can never thank him enough. He has been a great benefactor to me. I would like to repay the favour he has given me—but he is so self-sufficient, so well balanced, that he will never make the sort of silly mistake that I made.'

Amy muttered something. 'Everyone has their moments of lunacy, Sharla. Maybe you're lucky you made them early. You're wiser now, and won't make the same mistakes again.'

Sharla was herself too happy to notice Amy's glumness. 'You know, I feel like a million dollars, now that you all know about my little Shakira. Now I know it will not be too long before I can start being a real mother.' She caught Amy's hand. 'It was so lucky for me, the day Chris told me that he might have a job for me. And then I met you, and you were so very welcoming and nice to me—even though I was a stranger to you at first.' She walked to the window and looked out. The nights were drawing in now, and the mist was swirling in across the lake. Sharla thought it was beautiful, and said so. Amy saw only cold depression descending on her heart, but she tried to smile for her friend's sake.

It was Sharla herself who brought up Larry's name. 'He does not know I am once married?'

'I don't know. It won't make any difference to him. Why don't you tell him?'

She thought Sharla would rebel, but her eyes lit up. 'Oh yes, I must. I have to let him know that there is to be another small patient to put on his list.'

The mist came down, and dour clouds drifted slowly across the face of the moon, hiding the lake as it merged into the darkness of the trees. Amy gripped the window ledge until her knuckles were white. So this was what a broken heart felt like! She tried to tell herself that it would have been much worse if she had allowed herself to have an affair with Chris. But as the night darkened, so did her own spirits.

She heard George Bridges moaning in his room. Poor man, he hadn't much longer to go. She gave herself a mental shake, and said, 'I'd better get his mist euphoria.' She looked at the phial as she drew out the prescribed dose into a tiny cup. It worked for pain in the body. She held George's head gently as he drank, and stayed with him until he sank into a deep sleep, her hand gently on his thin white fingers.

CHAPTER TEN

AND SO Amy learned about love. Chris had gone away, back to the life he was destined for, the life he was best fitted for. And Amy found out what it was like to function with half of yourself missing. Everything she did in the course of a normal day reminded of him. When she sat and watched Edna Bell getting better, she thought of Chris. When she sat in the dining room and ate cottage pie, she thought of Chris. When she sailed, believing herself to be alone in the middle of the lake, it reminded her of Chris. But she sailed more, because in the middle of the lake with a wild autumn wind blowing, she knew that the challenge of keeping herself afloat matched the same challenge in her mental life.

Quintin, from being a pest and a nuisance, had become a friend, who talked about Chris in an intimate way, bringing closer home the friendship they had generated at school, at a time when Chris had lost his beloved mother, and felt a sudden sympathy with the underdog, with those to whom life had not been kind. Amy saw much more clearly how important Quintin's home had become to the growing boy with an image to keep up. It tore at her heart to think of the schoolboy, struggling not to show his distress, to pass his exams so that his father would be proud of him gaining entrance to medical college.

Quintin and Amy were thrown together even more, when Sharla decided to take a few days off to go down to see her daughter, to speak to the magistrate who was dealing with her case, and to drum up support from sympathetic friends and neighbours of her aunt.

It was Quintin who suggested one mild autumn morning that they both take the estate car and fulfil their promise to Chris to take a look at Four Winds, the house

at Kilderton that had been left to Chris and Veronica
jointly. Quintin confided, 'They've always got on. It's
just that Veronica has no maternal instincts—she
couldn't be a mother to him. But since Chris grew up,
they've been the best of friends. You'll see, she'll be
quite happy to sell her share of Four Winds to Chris.
Then I can get the contract to re-design it.'

'Why do you want to do that?' asked Amy.

'It's a family home. Chris won't want it. He and Fran
will live in London—maybe have a small villa in Antibes
later—they won't want to come back here. My plan is to
make it into two or maybe three luxury holiday flatlets.
There's land too—enough to put a caravan site on. I
think Chris would like that. If I can get the plans ready,
he just has to accept them—I know Chris. I'll have them
tailor-made—exactly what he wants.'

Amy was taken aback, but she hid it well. 'I suppose
there's no doubt that Veronica will want to sell?'

'No doubt. She hated it here. It was always raining,
and the social life was dire.'

'You don't think she ought to be consulted?'

'My dear girl, all I'm doing is looking around! Now
you heard Chris. That's exactly what he asked us to do,
right?'

'Well, yes, that's what he said, but——'

'Come on, Amy love, get the Ford out,' said Quintin
firmly.

'Why don't we ever use your car?' asked Amy.

'Because the roads are desperately muddy, love. It
would take me hours to clean the wheels.'

Amy smiled. She had learned tolerance, and she
found she could use it with everyone except Chris. 'Let's
go, maestro! I must confess I'm curious to see inside.'

'You'll be more curious to see my genius at work.
How to turn a Victorian monstrosity into a modern
ultra-fashionable block of pads for cool climbing cats.'

'What?'

'Climbers, Amy, climbers—the people who pay to
come to this godforsaken place, pay good money for

accommodation, for food and drink. Talking of drink, we'll have a pub lunch. I've already told Gwyn.'

Amy brought out the estate car. She had driven past Four Winds more than once, and knew the way well. It had drawn her, with the attraction of any lover for her loved one's associations. She drove quickly, excited at the thought of actually setting foot in the house where Chris was—not exactly the beloved only child, but certainly the only child.

Mrs Jolly was delighted to see them. 'My dears, come away in. I'm so glad young Dr Mac hasn't forgotten all about the place. Mrs Standish was here only a month ago. She was talking of having a party here at Christmas . . .'

'What? She didn't! She doesn't want it, surely?' Quintin was rattled.

Mrs Jolly might be a countrywoman, but she wasn't stupid. 'Nay, she doesn't want it, son. She just thought a house party might be a nice farewell thing to do. She hates the place—always has, unless it was full of her fashionable friends.'

Amy said, 'When will she let you know, Mrs Jolly?'

'I only hope in good time. I've things of my own to do at Christmas, that's for sure.'

'She would bring her own staff, would she?'

'If she comes, aye. I'd only have to keep it clean and aired.'

'Has she done that before?' asked Amy.

'Brought London staff?—aye, she has. Snooty lot they were too.'

Quintin pretended he hadn't heard that. 'Do you mind if I wander, Mrs Jolly? I'd like to get the feel of the place.'

Amy wanted to wander too, but Mrs Jolly detained her. 'And how are Miss Quayle and Miss Owens? I heard they weren't too good, poor dears.'

'Oh, they used to teach you in Kilderton school? I recall them talking of you. Yes, they aren't too bad just now. Doris—Miss Owens to you—has had some gall bladder problem, but nothing too serious.'

'Give them my kind regards,' said Mrs Jolly.

'You should call and visit. They'd be delighted.'

The women chatted for a while, until Quintin came down, bored. 'I say, Mrs Jolly, is there a key to the loft?' he asked.

She fetched it from a hook in the kitchen. 'I 'spect you think us country folk do nothing but gossip, happen?' She winked at Amy. 'Our little lives are maybe too small for you to be interested in. But when it's someone who first told me about China, and the Orient Express, and the Bluebell Girls and Queen Victoria's Jubilee . . . she opened our eyes for us, did Miss Owens.'

Amy did eventually get the chance to walk quietly by herself around Chris's house. The main thing she noticed was that there were no friendly ghosts. There were no ghosts. The house was totally uninhabited. And there was no sense of living and loving and having fun. It was a lonely house, still waiting after a hundred years for its first real family.

They would have left, but they heard the rattle of teacups in the next door cottage, and Mrs Jolly wouldn't dream of them leaving without a cup of coffee and a new-baked scone. And while she was boiling the kettle, Quintin made several rough sketches of Four Winds as he would like to see it. Amy watched, and felt sad that her dear Dr Mac's home wasn't a home at all.

They talked of Veronica as they sipped the coffee —freshly ground Blue Mountain. Mrs Jolly thought her a smart woman, with no harm in her, but not much use either. Which seemed probably a fair description, as far as being a stepmother and housewife was concerned.

'It still isn't too late. It would still make a lovely home. And the gardens could be beautiful. Did you see those lovely apple trees going to waste? And the space where someone planned a pond, but never actually got round to digging it?'

'Maybe I'll suggest that Chris and Francesca come up for a weekend—just to see if they like it,' said Quintin.

'Are they engaged?' Amy tried not to say it, but Quintin seemed sure that the two were already a couple.

'Well, she still has a long way to go in her career,' he said importantly. 'But they understand each other pretty well, and I think that's what matters in the long run, don't you?'

'He's never—mentioned—being interested in anyone else?'

'Not to me.'

Amy said nothing, but it reinforced her suspicions that she was nothing more to Chris than a pretty, expendable country girl—maybe interesting because of novelty value, but not interesting enough to intrude on his regular way of life. On the way back she clenched her fingers round the steering wheel, as she would like to clench them round Chris MacFarlane's neck if he ever brought the gorgeous Francesca anywhere near Kilderton.

Quintin didn't help, thinking aloud as they drove back in the increasing drizzle. 'Of course, since I've been in this area for some weeks now, I could always look around for a more suitable property for them, if they did have some fanciful ideas about having a place around here.'

When they got back to Greyrigg, Doris was poorly again, and Amy had to go straight up to her. 'Those pills Dr Mac gave me—they might be melting the stone, but they make me feel very ill sometimes, Amy. Are you sure he said to give me that many a day?'

Amy took no chances. Holding the box of ursodeoxycholic tablets, she phoned Larry's surgery. Larry seemed unwilling to go against Chris's orders. 'That man knows what he's doing,' he said. 'He did warn her that there'd probably be a few side-effects at first.'

'Larry, she doesn't look well,' said Amy anxiously.

'Halve the dose, then, until I see her. Unless you want to phone Chris?'

'No!' Amy had never been so emphatic. 'You know as much as he does. Why ring all the way to London?'

'All right, I'll pop in later.' Larry didn't sound too worried at the thought. Amy went back to Doris, where Martha was again keeping her company, and explained that the doctor was coming.

'But if you feel worse, let me know at once, Doris,' she told her.

She felt better when Larry did call. And Amy, after making sure all was well on a lower dosage, engineered that Sharla should come in from the physio wing just as Larry was on his way downstairs. Then she made herself suddenly very busy in the office, dictating letters to Faith Hindle. She heard the two talking in the hall, as Sharla saw him out. She heard Sharla's laughter—once a rare sound, but now so much more heard in the tall rooms of Greyrigg. It took Larry a good half hour to take his leave. Amy was secretly delighted. Sharla's problems were being ironed out with time, as she had hoped.

After Faith had finished and gone, Amy sat in the office, feeling a little chilly suddenly. Winter was approaching, after all. Maybe she should alter the central heating; there must be no chance of hypothermia among the Manor's old people. She heard a cry from upstairs—George Bridges again. Amy went up to sit with him. He seemed calmer when someone held his hand, talked to him, even though he was hardly strong enough to reply sometimes.

The days had not become much shorter when George died. It was a peaceful passing, with no pain. Daniel had gone to look for Frank Bates, who often took a night stroll unless closely supervised. He found him sitting holding George's hand, and called Amy, hearing George's breathing becoming irregular. It was a cold night, with the first suggestion of frost outside, the window frames glistening in the moonlight. Frank sat, his white hair lit by the moon, his hand on his friend's, with the same face of an angelic blankness that Amy remembered the day they had found him with the deer in the forest.

Amy was moved. She crept into the room, then

realised that George wasn't breathing. She took his other wrist, and felt for a pulse. There was none. She didn't move Frank yet. The room was warm, and he seemed content to stay, maybe until George's spirit had gone to find the end of his long life's journey.

The Manor was used to funerals. The last one had been Dr Mac's. Amy quietly and efficiently set things in motion, contacting the Canon and arranging a suitable date. The atmosphere was subdued but not grieving, for they were glad that George Bridges would suffer no longer.

Amy took out her fawn suit for the funeral; the grey one was for summer. The day dawned with the first real frost of the year, thick white icing over all the trees and shrubbery in the garden, and over the top of the mini-bus. Hannah had stayed on after doing night duty, to help with dressing the residents who wanted to come, and getting them all down to the dining room, where a cup of hot Bovril warmed both hands and insides before Arthur came round with the bus.

George had only one sister, and she and her young son were invited back to the Manor for lunch, then Sharla showed them the basketball team, and played some of the ballroom dance tapes—very quietly—to stop them feeling too sad.

The afternoon seemed to belie the fact that it was autumn. The sun blazed down, melting all the frost, lighting the gold, scarlet and russet in the forests to a show of beauty as magnificent as any Amy had ever seen. She changed into old clothes and walked down to the boatshed. It was time she took *Speedwell* out of the water. But when she arrived, the lake looked so inviting that instead of removing the mast and wrapping the tackle to keep in the Manor outbuildings for the winter, she actually set the sail, shaking out the remaining flakes of frost, and pushed off gently from the jetty into the cool rippling waters, the familiar lapping against her timbers.

The October sun reminded her of the July sun, except

that it was lower in the sky. And the perfect peace of the surroundings, the awful stillness of the fells and the gentle motion of the boat soothed her as it always did, and made her again thankful that she was one of the lucky ones, to spend her life among beauty and glory. The air was fresher than she had expected, and the wind was whipping up small wavelets, which had not been there when she set out. Never mind, a good sail, with the sheet pulling and the *Speedwell* showing what she could do, was the ideal way of spending a lonely afternoon. Amy sped across the water now, admiring the blue and purple of the fells, the gold and red of the trees, reflected in the broken surface of the lake.

The images around her touched her very soul. But an urgent puff of wind brought her back to reality suddenly, as the sheet was almost whipped out of her hand. She hauled on it quickly, regained control. She felt herself shiver, and wished she had put on more than just an anorak over her shirt. Her nose and ears began to feel as though they didn't belong to her. The bright sunny day was a smiling exterior for what she knew would soon be a treacherous spell of squally weather.

The tiller was suddenly almost snatched out of her hand. She stared at it, as though it were alive, as she grasped it more firmly, with fingers that were too cold to manipulate properly. The sail flapped as she lost the wind, and she had to struggle to regain control. She looked around. The fells that had once seemed merely majestic now looked too far away. She was right in the middle of the lake, and she decided it wasn't the best place to be in this kind of uncertain wind. The jetty seemed miles away—and when a gust hit the boat so suddenly that it keeled over, she knew it *was* miles away, as she gasped and sobbed in her efforts to stay afloat. She had always managed her *Speedwell* before. It had never seemed too much for her. A General Purpose dinghy was just right for a single sailor—though she had handled better with Chris on board, she recalled.

The sail was wet now, and sluggish to respond,

although she was gradually righting the craft. She flung all her weight the opposite way. The wind hit her, with an icy slap that felt as though it had come straight from the North Pole.

Amy looked hastily around. She had made very little progress towards the jetty. She gritted her teeth and made a determined effort to bring the boat to the position she wanted. She had never been beaten before. She wasn't going to allow herself to be overcome by a few squalls of playful wind. She reminded herself that she enjoyed a challenge—but this pleasure trip had suddenly become a terrifyingly menacing monster, struggling with her for her very life. The waves flung themselves into the boat, freezing her to the very marrow. And like the most enormous idiot she was, she had left the lifejacket before the mast, and hadn't bothered to put it on—the worst crime a sailor could commit.

Slowly, almost in slow motion, the sail descended to the level of the lake, and under it. Amy clung on to the side, her little weight pitifully inadequate with the drenched sail doubled in weight. Her eyes were closed, her breath bursting from her body as she clung with both hands on the sheet, willing the sail to lift from the water. Her legs were braced against the mast, the muscles aching with the effort and with the cold.

A voice said, 'Hold on, Amy! I've got you!'

She couldn't look round. She heard the voice again. 'I've got you.' And the gentle chugging of a small motor. She must be imagining it. But then strong arms seized her, and lifted her bodily into Farmer Crabtree's dinghy. Chris, meanwhile, transferred himself to the *Speedwell*, brought her upright with an enormous effort, ran down the sail and let it crumple inside the boat, then shouted to her to catch a tow. Amy dropped the rope at the first attempt. But her grit made her ignore the numbness in her hands, and she caught the tow and made it secure at the stern of the dinghy. Chris put up a thumb. 'Now get us back to port.'

She steered the dinghy, the gentle chug of its engine

one of the most welcome sounds she had ever heard. She was too bewildered and overcome to wonder why Chris had suddenly appeared. All that mattered now was that she made no more foolish mistakes, but brought the dinghy and *Speedwell* back to safety.

She switched off the engine, jumped out, and tied the dinghy securely. Chris followed her on to the rickety jetty, tying *Speedwell* firmly next to the dinghy. Amy turned towards Chris, as he dragged off his lifejacket and threw it into the boatshed. 'If you hadn't seen me, nobody knew I was out,' she said shakily. Her teeth were chattering, and she had never been so cold in her life.

'We won't go into that just now.' And he suddenly bent and picked her up, carrying her tight against his chest, as he covered the distance to the Manor more quickly than ever before. 'Damn this gate,' he muttered, as he tried to manipulate the kissing gate, and had to lift her over. Then it was up the drive to the Manor, calling out for someone to give him a hand.

Gwyn, Olive and Daniel, Sharla and Quintin were all there in a moment. Chris said curtly, 'I need a hot bath. Gwyn, tea, please—with sugar. Sharla, I'll need a hand upstairs. Get her bed ready and warm.'

Amy wanted to tell them that all this fuss wasn't necessary, but she found she couldn't speak. Her teeth seemed as though they would chatter for ever, and she felt terribly drowsy. And she knew that she had been in terrible danger.

She didn't know who undressed her, but the warm bath began to revive her, and she felt her hands and feet begin to come back to her. She slipped down in the bath, half asleep, and her head almost went under. But a hand caught her neck, and gently helped her out and into a warm thick towel. Her nightdress was pulled over her head, and a dressing gown. Her wet hair was towelled briskly. Then she was in her own warm bed, leaning back against extra pillows, and she felt warm and safe, and very, very tired.

She revived more when someone held a fragrant mug

of tea under her nose, and she was able to use her own hands to hold it, to savour the sweet hot liquid, that she could feel slipping down inside her, warming and reviving all through her body. Then she opened her eyes, as she heard Chris's voice. 'I'll have to take a look at you, Amy. Sit up, please.' He took the cup away from her. His stethoscope was already in his ears. She opened her mouth to protest, but no words came. She knew she needed a check-up—and Chris was the only doctor around. She took a deep breath as he sat on the bed beside her and himself took off her dressing gown and pulled down her nightdress straps.

She had come back to consciousness with a bang. But Chris's face was totally professional as he listened carefully to her heartbeats. She wondered what message they were giving him, knowing how she was conscious of them whenever he was near. He listened carefully to her lungs, both front and back. She tried not to look at his clear, sensible eyes as he moved the instrument over her chest and asked her to breathe in deeply. He had saved her life.

'All right, no harm done. You can finish your tea now.' And as he pulled her straps back for her, and put the dressing gown round her shoulders, his head was very close to hers, and she fancied his lips brushed against her naked shoulder before he covered it with the gown.

Ruth Taylor came in. 'I took that one away, doctor. We've made you a fresh pot.' And she placed a tray with two cups of tea beside them, and a plate of newly baked scones.

Chris gave Amy a one-sided grin. 'Shall I be mother?'

She accepted the cup, refused anything to eat. 'I want to know how you were there. I'll never understand how I didn't die. I know I was praying, but I didn't think I deserved such an answer. It's too enormous a thing to accept, you being there, just when I needed you so much.'

A tear slid from her eye, down her cheek, and into her

teacup. Chris took the cup from her. 'It isn't really a miracle, Amy. I heard about George's funeral, and I tried to get up in time. But there was a big accident on the motorway, and because we were diverted, I was late, and was only just driving round the lake when I recognised *Speedwell* and stopped to watch. I saw the wind getting up. It was so quick, I thought I'd never get there in time.' He put a hand over hers, his voice suddenly rather hoarse.

'You saw the wind coming?' queried Amy.

'I saw it before you did. I saw the water being whipped up in front of the squall. The whole lake turned grey, and I knew you hadn't seen it. I was in that dinghy before you capsized.'

'Thank God, thank God!'

'Thank Him indeed. Another five minutes, and I might have been too late.'

'I was very foolish,' she admitted. 'I don't usually go out unprepared. I suppose I was a bit depressed after the funeral.'

'You have a lot on your mind.'

She looked sharply at him then. Was he going to say she was doing too much—that she had taken on too much by insisting on doing the improvements her own way? She met his gaze then, and a most beautiful and gentle smile started in his eyes, and spread to his lips, a smile too kind and too sincere not to respond to. 'You're too nice to say it. But I'll admit that life has been rather hectic for me recently. I've always enjoyed a challenge. I suppose I did do too much.'

'You can cope, my dear—I can see that. But have you realised that apart from the two days I made you stay in London, you've had no time off whatsoever? That's wrong, Amy. Everyone has to have a holiday. Promise me you'll take a break as soon as possible?'

'I will. I was cheeky ever to think of arguing with you.' She felt very sleepy suddenly, but wanted him to know the truth before she fell completely asleep.

And though her eyes were closed, she heard his

murmur, 'No, Amy, not cheeky. I admired you for it, truly I did.'

'Will you be staying?'

Her words were whispered by now, but he heard them. 'I can't. I have to get back tonight—I'm sorry.'

And two tears tried to escape from her closed eyelids, before she slept, and felt warm and comfortable again, but very alone . . .

She didn't wake until morning. Sharla came in with a smile, fully dressed. 'I went for the papers, Amy. No need to stir.'

'I feel fine, truly,' Amy assured her.

'Have breakfast in bed, then.'

'Has Chris gone?' asked Amy.

'Yes. He had an important meeting at the Royal College. The Prince of Wales was going to speak.' Sharla drew back the curtains, showing a misty but sunny morning. 'He's one of the important ones—committee or something. Has to be there. It was sweet of him to come for the funeral, though.'

'He's like that.'

Sharla turned and looked at Amy, her dark eyes warm and understanding. 'Now you know how I feel.'

Amy said nothing. Nobody would ever know how she felt, because she would not let anyone know how in love she was. She would stay friends with Chris. Every time he came to Greyrigg, they would chat like old friends, get on well . . . and then he would go back to his life, and she would go on with hers . . . She smiled a sad smile. It sounded very Victorian to do that. Surely it would make more sense to allow herself to have an affair with him? She hadn't wanted that before. But now that she saw how their lives would be, she decided to herself that next time Chris MacFarlane came to visit, she would take his love, give hers in return, even though it wouldn't last, and there could never be more than an affair between them.

She lay back on the pillows, satisfied with her decision. 'Next time . . .'

Sharla said, 'What did you say?'

'Nothing. You don't know when Chris is coming again?'

'No. He's going away for Christmas. Maybe in the New Year.'

'Okay.' I can wait. It will be worth waiting for. I'll tell him, when he comes. I won't fight shy of him, and I won't nag. I'll show him how I love him. He won't be mine, exactly—but he will belong to me in a tiny way, one part of him will be mine . . .

'You know, he asked me to tell you something,' said Sharla.

'What?' Amy sat up then. Ruth was bringing her breakfast in, and Sharla was standing at the door, ready to go down. 'What did he say? Tell me, Sharla! I'll do anything for him, now that my life is all owed to him.'

Her friend smiled. 'He said you weren't to go back to work until you'd taken at least a week off.'

'Oh, rubbish! I've got too much to do. And I must let Dandy Hall know that we can take three new residents. If she wants, we can have them in before Christmas. And if Shakira comes too, we'll have such a lovely house-party that we won't even notice that Chris isn't with us.'

Sharla looked at her. Amy was being too cheerful. From her face, it was obvious she had just learned Amy's secret, but Sharla kept quiet. It would do no good at all to say anything just now. 'Get some rest today, Amy,' she advised.

Amy lay back on the pillows again, her eyes already closing. The experience had indeed been a big one. She needed to rest, and time to get used to her one big special idea . . .

CHAPTER ELEVEN

THE SNOW came early that year. Amy woke to a strange brightness in her room, an almost eerie silence from the farm rooster, and knew that the first snow had come. She jumped out of bed—not exhilarated by its beauty, but frightened by its suddenness, knowing that the freezer wasn't stocked up against bad weather, the emergency generator had not been serviced, and she hadn't checked up on their medicine chest.

Mr Gately was inclined to be cheerful. 'Nay, it's come to nowt, this early. This time next week there'll be nowt left but on top of Helvellyn and Gable.'

'All the same, I like to be ready. Is Farmer Williams' wholesale meat place open yet?'

Mr Gately shook his head. 'Not when I passed. Happen he'll be doing a few killings now—folk'll be ordering, no doubt, ready for winter.'

'Including me.' Amy picked up her papers. 'Come on, Nell.'

'I hear your London chappie's gone,' remarked Mr Gately. 'Funny lad, he was, but not a bad chap when you got to know him.'

Amy smiled. 'Not a bad chap.' Quintin's departure had been hastened by the imminent arrival of Sharla's baby. Sharla was being moved to the big room, so that there was plenty of room for Shakira's cot. 'You know we're getting a new resident? A seven-month baby, daughter of our physiotherapist.'

'Well now! That's a grand piece of news.' Mr Gately was intrigued, as the main purveyor of gossip. 'And is the daddy coming too?'

'The daddy has got himself a divorce.' Amy knew the word would be spread, so she decided it better be the correct version, and not tittle-tattle. 'He wasn't the home-loving type—went off with someone else while his wife was pregnant.'

'Ee, now, bless her. I'm that glad she's found a bit of peace at Manor. Nice young woman too. Very nice.'

Yes, very nice. And so happy and cheerful now, full of energy at her job, and enjoying the dancing as well as the basketball with her 'class' in the afternoons before tea. The Manor was usually full of music and fun these days, thanks to Sharla's unfailing liveliness. She had seen Shakira twice, and a big reception was planned for the little mite. Auntie Mira was coming with her as nanny, which suited everyone, especially Mira, who had no other relatives in Britain.

When Amy got back, Daniel and Olive were just finishing their breakfast, and she joined them in the big kitchen. 'Nice and cosy, since we had the insulation in?' she asked.

'Aye, you could say that. I were never so pleased as when young Quintin took his fancy plans away with him.' Gwyn looked around the comfortable room. 'Now I've got my new cooker, all we need is the freezer doing.'

'I'll see to it this morning,' promised Amy.

Daniel said, 'And the medicines. Remember last year?'

Sharla had come in. 'Hello, everyone. What happened last year? This snow is beautiful.'

'Beautiful but deadly.' Amy shivered at the memory. 'The road to town was blocked, and we'd forgotten to stock up on GNT.'

Sharla opened her eyes. 'Just about the most useful drug in the cupboard.'

Amy said, 'There was an empty pack that I thought was full. Anyway, I swore never to be so low again. We had to get the mountain rescue helicopter to deliver emergency supplies.' She poured coffee for Sharla. 'Looking forward to tomorrow?'

'Oh dear, I hope the train bringing Shakira won't be held up by snow.'

Amy quoted Mr Gately. 'Not when it comes early.

Look, the clouds are all gone. Don't worry, Sharla
—we'll organise a back-up team.'

They went together to take tea to the guests, and when
Amy had said good morning to them, she settled down
to a morning of organisation—the generator man first.
He promised to come that afternoon. Then a word with
Stanley King, the pharmacist, with a list of drugs they
would need. 'Young Dr Ford will come and give me
prescriptions for all these?' he queried.

'Yes. He'll be coming today,' said Amy. 'I'll ring him
and ask him to call and pick them up on his way. The
road is quite passable, is it?'

'The ploughs have been round. You should have no
bother.'

Farmer Williams was helpful too. 'I'd better deliver
while we can get round, Amy love. All right if I get
Charlie to bring a couple of lambs and a side of beef
across in boat? Arthur be able to meet him at jetty?'

'Thank you, Mr Williams. I don't intend to be caught
out this year.'

'Don't hesitate if your stocks get low,' he told her. 'I'll
probably have to have the helicopter for High Wood
Farm cottages. It's not that much bother, lass.'

'Thank you. I'll give Arthur a cheque when he comes
to meet the boat.'

After lunch, in their quiet time, Amy and Sharla
moved Sharla's things to the room that had been
Quintin's, and before that, old Dr Mac's. Amy sat back
and admired their handiwork. 'We've seen some
changes this year,' she remarked. 'I was sad at first. And
boy, did I dislike you and Quintin for coming down when
you weren't wanted!'

Sharla said, 'It wasn't obvious. You were very sweet at
the funeral. Chris was most impressed.'

Amy went to the window, remembering again that
blazing sun that had made Chris shade his eyes as he
faced her across that newly-dug grave, the soil powdery
in the heat. For a moment the snowy garden vanished,
and she saw only the lush green yews, the Jaguar and the

Lancia and the white BMW in the drive, when they had
all come back for Gwyn's vol-au-vents and oatmeal
biscuits . . .

Her vision was blotted out by the very real arrival,
with chained wheels and wearing a sheepskin coat, of
Larry Ford in his Land Rover. Sharla heard the sound of
his engine, and her eyes brightened. 'Is that Larry with
the drug shopping list?'

'Yes. Would you mind checking it with him—please
make sure I haven't forgotten anything?'

'Right.' Sharla didn't ask why Amy didn't come
with her to meet the doctor. She flew down the steps, her
feet scarcely touching them, and arrived at the door
just as Larry pushed it open and called, 'Anyone
home?'

Amy finished straightening Sharla's pretty flowered
duvet, stopped for a moment to admire the baby's
matching coverlet, with the woollen toys and cuddly
dolls made by some of the old ladies as soon as they knew
Shakira was coming. She had hidden a fresh orchid in
her own room, and now she carried it in, a wonderful
blushing pink and white, to match the covers, and put it
on the dressing table, with a little card saying 'Welcome,
Sharla and Shakira'.

They had arranged for Aunt Mira to sleep next door.
The maids had already changed the bed and put up fresh
curtains, but Amy took a little posy of flowers there too,
a bunch of yellow and white chrysanthemums with
feathery fern.

There had been no reason for Larry to call today. No
one was ill, touch wood, and he had seen everyone only
three days ago. When he had called yesterday to say he
would visit, Amy couldn't help feeling that there was
more to the visit than purely professional diligence. She
heard their voices downstairs. Sharla had made a pot of
tea, and they had taken it into the deserted dining room.
The door was almost closed. Amy decided that she had
no reason to go in there, and went to chat to Olive and
Gerry.

Olive said as soon as she entered the lounge, 'I do hope she says yes.'

Amy tried to look stern—and failed. 'It's none of our business,' she said firmly.

'Oh, come on—with a long winter ahead, with coughs and bronchitis and maybe pneumonias and 'flu? Give us a break, Amy! Let us dream of a winter romance: Love in the Snow. You can't blame us for wanting to cheer up the days ahead.'

'I suppose not. But don't be too eager, you might embarrass them.'

Gerry stood up. 'I say, they've gone for a walk in the garden. That's a bit obvious, isn't it? Two sets of foot-prints off into the shrubbery?'

'Come back!' But Amy took a little peep herself. It did suggest romance. And the footprints were close together, as though the two were walking arm in arm.

Olive said, 'The signs were there, you know, for all to see. Why did he come out with Biddy's eardrops, when the chemist was calling that day? Why does he visit twice a day after surgery? Surely he knows that everyone is okay. No, the question is to be popped, I'll bet on it.'

The concealed excitement mounted, as Sharla and Larry did not return from the garden. There was a pale sun out, but it could hardly be said to be working weather. Amy gazed rather sentimentally at the foot-prints, beginning to melt round the edges. Good luck, Sharla, she thought. Better luck than last time.

Olive's squeak heralded the return of the couple. Amy stood back from the window, but she could see enough. Sharla and Larry were indeed linking arms —there quite clearly existed nothing else in the world for them at that moment but each other. Olive said, 'Some-one's got to go. They've got to tell someone, or we'll all burst!'

'Don't be inelegant!' But Amy went out into the hall as Larry was stamping the snow from his boots outside. 'Hi, Larry. Sorry I wasn't here to meet you. Everything all right?'

'Fine, thanks.' He looked shy but proud, his face flushed with perhaps more than just the chill of the day. 'Just one small problem, Amy.'

'Anything I can help with?'

'Can you find a suitable date for a wedding? Sharla has agreed to marry me.' He took her hand in his, and they faced Amy and the others. 'We don't want to get in the way of Christmas. And we don't want to wait either. And naturally, we want absolutely everybody to come.'

Amy went to Sharla and hugged her hard. Then she kissed Larry on the cheek, and shook his hand hard. 'There's no problem. Three weeks for the banns—how about December the first?'

Larry said, 'To be honest, I don't know much about weddings. I'd love to be selfish and leave all the arrangements to you.'

Sharla put in, 'That is, if you don't mind, Amy.'

Olive and Gerry had finished congratulating the couple. Gerry said, 'She would have been furious if you hadn't asked her.'

Amy joined in the laughter. 'Let's sit down and make lots of lists. That's what I always do when I don't know where to start.'

No one would have guessed that it was a dull, cold day. Inside the Manor there was excitement and happiness and a great deal of talk. They arranged the church service and spoke to Canon Forrester. They made a guest list—not large, as Sharla only had her Aunt Mira, who would be here soon, and Larry's parents were his only family. 'And you'll need a best man, Larry,' they reminded him.

'I'd say there was no argument about that—Chris, if he'll come. It was Chris who introduced us.'

Amy tried to still her palpitations. 'If he's in the country. Can I leave you to contact him?'

'Yes, indeed. I'll phone this evening.'

Amy went back to her list. 'Sharla, any bridesmaids?'

'I had not even thought. How many does one usually have?'

'Two or three, I suppose. Someone must hold your bouquet during the ceremony.'

'Will you do it, Amy?'

'I'd love to. Anyone else?'

Sharla smiled. 'Could I be very boastful and ask Edna? She is almost walking unaided. If I tell her she is to walk up the aisle—even though it is only a little one, I know it will be the spur I need to make her succeed.'

Amy smiled and wrote down Amy Taggart and Edna Bell. 'Anyone else?'

Sharla thought. 'It would be nice to ask Aggie Brown.'

Amy wrote down the name. 'It would also be diplomatic, or she might decide to faint in the aisle to get attention!' She looked up. 'Well, Sharla, all you have to do now is ask them.'

Larry looked at his watch. 'Good lord, it's dark already! I'll be late for evening surgery.' Sharla went to the door with him. The others continued far into the evening, with the enchanting talk of flowers and veils, of white lace and golden rings. While they talked, the snow began to fall again silently, re-covering the ground where it had melted during the brief spell of sunshine.

'And someone must give you away,' Amy reminded Sharla.

'My parents are dead.'

'Any friend? How about Quintin?'

Sharla smiled. 'No. Quintin is nice, but I'd like someone from here. Do you think the Major would do that for me?'

Amy laughed with sheer delight. 'Sharla, you're doing exactly what I did! You've adopted my family to be yours as well. The Major will be over the moon! He can wear his medals. And he should be off his crutches in a couple of weeks. His new hip will make his military bearing even grander.'

It was only at bedtime that Amy remembered that the generator man had not come. Oh well, he would come tomorrow. She went to bed, like most of the other souls under her care, in a rosy haze of pleasure and anticipation.

Aggie couldn't sleep, and had to be given a sleeping tablet. 'What do bridesmaids wear in winter?' she wanted to know.

'We can decide that tomorrow.'

'Peggy Bickerstaffe used to be a seamstress for the Co-op. I think we ought to have a word with her tomorrow.' Aggie sounded very important. 'And it's ages since I had my hair done, lass. Can you get it fixed up in time?'

Amy went down to her office to lock up for the night. The big calendar on the wall, the one with all the winners of the sheepdog trials, was empty for December. She circled the first with a bold red circle and drew a heart inside it.

The telephone rang. She picked it up quickly, as it was late, and she didn't want anyone to be woken. 'That was quick, Amy Taggart,' said a well-known voice.

'Hello, Chris.' Her heart thumped painfully, and she fought to control it. 'Larry has told you, then.'

'Yes. Great news, eh? I couldn't be more delighted.'

'They're very good for each other. You will be able to come, then? No winter sports, or such things?'

'Don't be sarcastic!' he laughed.

'I wasn't. I just got the impression that you always went away when the weather got worse.' She didn't want to quarrel with him any more. She had made her decision. If she were lucky enough still to have his affection, she was going to make sure she said nothing to lose it.

'I'm not going away.' His tone was curt. 'And I suppose you didn't take my professional advice and take a holiday either?'

'I couldn't, Chris. I had to organise things for the bad weather. I'm still waiting for the generator man, and the meat is being delivered for the deep-freeze.'

'Look, Amy, I'd like to give them a really nice present. Can you think of anything they'd like?'

'To be honest, once Shakira is here, Sharla wants nothing else in the world,' Amy told him.

'Shakira!' That gave him an idea. 'Why don't we take out a policy for the baby? That would mean that even if Sharla stopped working, there would be something coming to Shakira later. Will you join me?'

'Yes, if you like. I'm sure it's a good idea.'

'And don't be offended if I say I can afford a little more than you.'

Amy swallowed. This was the moment when she showed him she had changed. 'I won't. I told you, the day you saved my life, I won't argue with you again. And I'm sorry I did when I first knew you.'

'Apology accepted, Amy Taggart. But—oh well, it doesn't matter——'

'Go on with what you were going to say,' she invited.

'It can wait.' There was a pause. 'I'm sure you'll organise everything beautifully. I promise I won't lose the ring.'

'I know you won't,' said Amy. 'You do everything right.'

'Hmm. Are you sure you aren't making fun of me?'

'*Now* who can't do anything right? You're annoyed if I argue! Now you're puzzled because I don't. What would please you, Chris? Do you know?'

He gave a little laugh, without mirth. 'I'm not as certain as I was.'

She took that to mean that he wasn't as fond of her as he used to be, and accepted it with good grace. Maybe things were better that way. She had left it too late to be nice to him. It was her own fault now. They would be standing side by side in the tiny church. She would be holding the bride's bouquet, and Chris would be looking as dashing as he had ever done. And there would be nothing left between them but polite nothings . . .

'Are you still there, Amy?'

'Yes.'

'Quint said you saw Four Winds together?'

'Yes. He wants to make flats.'

'And you?'

'It's none of my business, but it's a fine family home. It seems a shame to take away its chance. The garden is big, and there are apple trees and a place for a pond——'

'I remember—I did that! I started to make a pond, but there wasn't the time.'

She said quietly, 'Maybe some other little boy might like to finish it.'

'You're right. See you in December, then, Amy Taggart.'

What could she say that would show him she cared? 'Yes. I—I hope——' she began.

'Go on?'

'I—can't.' And she flung the receiver back on the rest before the tears came. What a fool she was! What a silly, lovesick fool. He would have guessed, and he would pity her. And she didn't want that. Amy trailed upstairs, her feet leaden as her heart. She didn't want to be smart and sophisticated, but it would have been nice to find just a few suitable words to say, instead of dissolving into unsophisticated tears.

When she spoke to Larry next day, he was overjoyed. 'Chris couldn't have been nicer—said that wild horses, snow blizzards and Old Nick himself wouldn't keep him away from the wedding!' They were together at the Manor. Sharla had gone with Arthur and Ruth Taylor in the estate car, to bring Shakira and Mira from the station. It had been decided to stay out of the way until the child got used to being somewhere new.

Larry said, 'You do understand, Amy—about—us——?'

She knew what he was trying to say. 'You and I have always been friends, but only friends, right? I hope it goes on like that.'

'I'll not forget how you helped us to get together. Neither will Sharla. She says you're like a sister to her,' said Larry earnestly.

Amy hid her emotion. 'Well, as we've both adopted

the residents for a family, it does make us sort of related, doesn't it?'

'Are you happy to have Shakira here?' he asked.

'Very happy. And she and Mira can stay while you go off on a wonderful honeymoon. Plans after that will have to wait. We'll have all the time in the world to sort things out.'

'The honeymoon! I forgot!' Larry exclaimed. 'I'll have to book it soon. Gosh, Amy, what shall I do?'

'Don't flap, Larry. Just call in at the travel agents tomorrow. They'll find you something nice.'

'I was wondering whether Sharla would like to go to Kashmir?'

'Wow!' exclaimed Amy.

'My parents have offered to pay. We must talk it over soon. I just want to give Sharla a nice time—she's suffered enough for one lifetime.' And Amy saw such a light in his eyes that she turned away a little, to hide her momentary envy of her friend's happiness.

She lay in bed that night, listening to the silence, knowing that the snow was coming down again. But now she had completed all she had to. The Manor was insulated and warm. The electricity was serviced, the freezer full. All drug supplies had been replenished. And most important of all, little Shakira was back with her mother, sleeping cosily in the cot in Dr Mac's old room.

Sharla brought the baby to meet the residents next morning after breakfast. The nurses brought everyone into the lounge, while Mira and Sharla were bathing Shakira. There was great expectation and much reminiscing about grandchildren of their own. Sarah-Jane reminisced about royal babies she had seen being taken for walks in royal parks, and was called names by Aggie Brown for being stuck-up.

Fortunately, the quarrel was interrupted by the arrival of the proud mother. Shyly she walked in, holding the child close, her cheek against Shakira's paler one. 'This is my baby,' she announced. She sat down, and turned

Shakira round so that everyone could see her face. The big dark eyes stared, and Amy thought she would cry. But as soon as the baby saw everyone, she looked back to reassure herself that Sharla was there, then gave the most beautiful smile, showing two teeth up and down. Her hair was dark brown and curly, and there was a lot of it, giving her an older look than a European baby of seven months.

The chorus of oohs and ahs made Sharla smile. She managed the baby well, with no sign that at the beginning of the little life she had become so depressed she didn't want to look after her.

'I was hoping Larry would come too—but he did say hello last night. I suppose the roads are so bad that he is taking a long time over calls.'

Sarah-Jane Phelps turned her wheelchair right round, so that she could see Shakira properly. She didn't wear glasses, even at ninety-nine. Her usually haughty face softened into a smile as she gazed. 'Oh, little one, what a long long time since I was your age! God bless you, my dear.'

Shakira was so even-tempered that she sat contented on her mother's knee, showing no sign that she wanted to leave. But Sharla was anxious that she learn to keep regular hours at the Manor. She was just lifting her to take her back to bed when the sound of Larry's engine could be heard struggling up the drive. Arthur had shovelled the snow aside, but it was still thick and difficult to manoeuvre. Sharla ran to the window, and made Shakira wave a small hand at the smiling young doctor.

He came in with a rush. 'Sorry I'm late, but I stopped to bring this.' And to everyone's delight, he slipped a solitaire diamond ring on to Sharla's slim brown finger. 'Almost forgot,' he confessed. 'I hope you'll put me right if I slip up on etiquette. Major, I know you will. Miss Phelps, I hope I can rely on you?'

The Major chuckled. 'Just don't forget her birthday, my boy, and you'll survive!'

Damaris Jarvis stood up, clearing her throat. She was a simple countrywoman, but somehow she was the best to make a speech on behalf of them all. 'Doctor—Sharla —we do appreciate you sharing your happiness with us. I want to say from the bottom of my heart that we all hope you stay as happy as we can see you are today.'

Amy blinked back a tear as they all clapped. Then Sharla went away to put the baby to bed, before coming back to let everyone see her shining diamond. She was grateful to Aggie Brown for dragging their attention to a matter close to her own heart. 'Amy, you do know that we only have three weeks to make our dresses?' she pointed out.

Sharla and Amy sat down, as an earnest discussion was obviously about to take place. 'Red is the colour of marriages in my country,' Sharla told Amy. 'I will wear white, naturally, because my fiancé wants me to, but I thought we could all carry red roses, tied with silver.'

'Red doesn't suit me.' Aggie was nothing if not direct.

Edna Bell protested, 'I'm sure it does, Agnes, with your white hair. I love the idea of red myself. Velvet would be nice.'

'Ugh!' Aggie pulled a face. 'It sounds like a Sunday school picnic with white pinafores!'

Sharla said, 'Why not white blouses?' And so the subject continued, with advice from Peggy Bickerstaffe and Sarah-Jane and others, showing that age never changes the feminine interest in dressing up.

'Don't forget, when the skirts are made, that Aggie's will need to be longer at the back, because of her stoop.'

'I do not stoop, Damaris Jarvis! I never stoop.'

'You do, you vain old thing. It's just that you stand up straight when you look at yourself in the mirror. As soon as you stop seeing yourself, you stoop.'

Amy had to intervene. 'Let's not argue. The dress-maker will decide on the hemlines. I suppose roses will be expensive in December.' She made notes in the notebook she kept in her pocket these days. There was so much going on that she had to make sure she forgot nothing. Chris had been right—it was a bit of a strain, and as she walked back to the office that evening, for the first time she felt tired, and the spring had gone from her step.

'The music!' Sharla came running after her. 'I forgot —I am supposed to choose two hymns. Can you help me, Amy? I am not sure which to choose.'

Amy made a note. 'We'll talk in the morning.'

'And are you sending Quintin an invitation?'

'I will, yes.'

'Only I think he said he was going to Barbados in December.'

Amy made another note. 'I'll telephone first,' she decided.

The phone rang. 'Hello?' It was Dandy Hall. 'Amy, could I ask you to take three new people? Two men and a lady with a parrot?'

'What? A parrot?' Sharla grinned at the conversation, as Amy went on, 'I'm honestly not sure about the parrot. We have a baby here. And a collie.'

'She's a very well-behaved parrot,' Dandy assured her.

'Come and see me tomorrow, Dandy, and we'll see what we can do.' Amy put the phone back, smiling and yawning at the same time. 'Oh well, we can manage three more. I suppose. Remind me to send them an invitation to the wedding.'

Sharla picked up a pencil and added the note herself, to Amy's long list of things needing attention. 'I'll go up now, Amy, unless you need me,' she said.

'No, you go, Shakira's mum. I'll be up in a few minutes now. Just the doors to lock.'

Amy was replacing the big keys behind the office door when the phone rang again. 'Hello?' she said.

'Is that Amy Taggart?' A woman's voice, youngish, plummy.

'Speaking.'

'This is Francesca Forbes. Amy, I want you to leave Chris alone. It's doing him no good at all, this affair of yours. He was happy enough until he met you. Now he's all fidgety, and he's never available when I want him.'

Amy's lips set together. 'Oh, what a shame!' she said mockingly.

'No, it's not like that. What I wanted to say was that he isn't himself. You making him drive up there so often isn't good for him. Can't you see? He just isn't your type. And now he's even cancelled our holiday. He needs his holidays, Amy. He's a professional man.'

'He didn't tell you why he'd cancelled the holiday?' asked Amy.

'No, but I bet he's coming up to see you again.'

Amy disliked the petulant, spoiled voice at the other end of the line. And she could be as direct as Aggie Brown if she felt the urge. 'And you think that will ruin his life?'

'I know it will. I'm asking for sacrifice from you. I ask it for his sake.' Francesca was acting now, her voice trembling in sham compassion.

Amy began to enjoy herself. If she couldn't have Chris in person, she would have a fantasy Chris, who adored her, and couldn't stay away from Greyrigg Manor. 'I'll tell you what I'll do, Francesca—I'll ask him to choose between us, shall I?' She said it with such confidence, as though she knew that she had Chris MacFarlane under her thumb. 'A free choice?'

'No!' And then the voice tried to be conciliatory. 'That would be childish. We both know that Chris isn't ready to settle down yet.'

'You may,' said Amy. 'But I have no intention of not seeing him, in that case. As long as he wants me, I'm here. My life is his, my love is his, whenever and wherever we both are. Is that clear?'

The reply was angry and shrill. 'I think you're a selfish bitch! I can't see what Chris sees in you. Or Quintin. They must both be out of their minds!' And Francesca slammed the phone down.

Amy smiled at first. So much for being naïve and unsophisticated! She had handled that woman as she

deserved to be handled, and she felt marginally more
pleased with herself. But as she trailed upstairs in the
darkness of the night, with the blanket of snow around
the still Manor, she knew that it was only makebelieve,
and that the blanket of snow lay around her own heart as
well. And she began to feel sorry for Francesca. They
probably both had a rival now. She ought to have
sympathised with her.

CHAPTER TWELVE

NEXT morning the snow lay deep, but it had stopped falling. The sunlight was blinding on the fallen drifts. Amy got up late. She had heard Sharla running down the drive, calling Nell to follow her. She had the joy, the energy—the luck. Amy lay back, trying not to think about the advice that had been given her—'You must take a holiday. You need a break.' So she had a ten-minute break, allowing Sharla to go for the papers.

She joined the others for breakfast, reluctant to let them see her depression. So she joked, and laughed, and looked forward to the wedding. It was difficult to keep it convincing, but she tried. It was Hannah who came into the kitchen, bent and whispered in Amy's ear, 'Doris is bad again.'

Sharla was laughing, telling everyone how Billy Braithwaite had been surprised to see a different female taking Nell for the papers. 'But I beat him. He has challenged me to a re-match, but I told him I was getting married soon, and had to save my strength.'

Under cover of the gale of laughter, Amy slipped away. Doris Owens was doubled up in pain, and there was no way she could leave her to suffer. 'Hang on, Doris. I'll get you in to see the surgeons. Ruth, pack her a hospital bag. Toothbrush, towel, spare nightie . . .' Amy was efficient. She had Arthur and Daniel get Doris to the car, and at the same time, sent a message to Sharla to let the hospital admissions know she was coming. Doris had tried the alternative treatment faithfully, but it hadn't worked. Amy was in love with the physician, but if his treatment wasn't working, then she had to find someone else—fast.

Sharla came running out. 'The road is blocked—there was a fall in the night.' But Amy had no time to wait.

Doris lay on the back seat, trying not to groan. Sharla's message was helpful, but she still had to go. If Billy had reported a fall of snow, then by now it was probably cleared away.

She set off. In the background she heard the strains of the Military Twostep; Sharla had started her ballroom dancing class early. She negotiated the drive, that Arthur had cleared with geometric precision. The lumps of snow lay in chiselled heaps on each side of the drive. The side where the daffodils and snowdrops would eventually appear, in their annual miracle.

Amy had not requested an ambulance from the hospital; they liked to keep some in reserve. And there was always the 'bank' of private people willing to be called out in an emergency. She regarded herself as part of the 'bank', and took her own patients in whenever possible. But as she drove along the snowy road, she began to wonder if she had done the right thing. Doris was very ill. Although she was aware of the diagnosis, there was still a lot of human suffering going on before help was forthcoming. Amy kept looking back. She could see from Doris's face that the pain was severe.

She was cheered by the sight of a farm tractor ahead. It would act like a snowplough, and clear the road for her. It was slow but sure progress. She had time to notice how the sunlight on the lake looked like clusters of diamonds. And though the sun was bright, there was no heat in it, the car heater giving out very little warmth at such a slow speed.

The tractor turned off, and Amy speeded up a little —until, rounding a bend, she came to what she had feared most—a slip of snow across the road. There were three workmen and a Council lorry already shovelling as hard as they could. With a word of encouragement to Doris, Amy jumped out, took her spade from the back, and set to clear a way. 'I've got a sick woman in the car. We must get her to Kendal,' she explained.

'Better go back and phone for someone to meet you here,' the men advised.

Amy puffed as she dug. 'It'll take longer to go back. Come on, I only need enough for a little car. Keep digging!' She had put on a scarf and gloves, but soon discarded them as her cheeks glowed from the exercise. She wouldn't give up. Four of them could get through. Amy's own energy and determination shamed the men, who started working more quickly.

'You're Warden at Greyrigg,' said one of them. 'I've seen you at church.'

'I am,' she smiled.

'I must say you've plenty of beef for a little lass.' And he put his back into the task, muttering about the snowplough being always somewhere else when you needed it. The lake was on one side of the small road, a solid wall of rock on the other. But slowly they began to see the way through. 'Get back in, lass. You'll get through now. Go carefully, mind. And good luck to you!'

'Let's hope there isn't another fall when I come back!'

'Nay, we'll have plough by then.' The men waved as Amy triumphantly negotiated the snow slip and set off towards Kilderton. Even Doris managed a small cheer.

The roads were clearer near Kilderton. Then there was a stretch of dual carriageway which needed a little care because it was slippery. The gritting lorries were out, but there were not enough of them. Once in Kendal, the way was clear. The AED porters and a Sister were waiting, and Doris was admitted with the minimum of fuss. She wouldn't let Amy wait. 'Get back to the Manor, love. They'll let you know how I get on.' She tried to smile. 'I just hope I don't miss the wedding.'

'I promise to bring you out for it.' Amy left her in the ward, and hurried back to the car. She was cold now, and blew on her fingers before getting back at the wheel. But her main worry was meeting that bad patch on the lakeside road. Her heart lifted when she saw it was still clear enough to pass by, and there were warning signs, telling motorists that the road was closed except for access. She accelerated once she was past the danger spot, and arrived back at the Manor with a spurt, getting out feeling triumphant as well as hungry.

The dressmaker had come out to fit the red velvet skirts, and she was doing it in the lounge, to the delight of all the residents. Peggy Bickerstaffe was proving that she still knew her trade, and was helping with the pinning and the advice, looking years younger because she had something to do. Sharla was there too. 'You see what I mean, Amy? This is what the ballroom dancing does. Their eyes really light up when they feel they are doing something well.'

'Pity we can't have more weddings, then,' laughed Amy.

'Well, there's still you to marry off.'

'I'm one of life's bachelor girls,' said Amy firmly.

'Nonsense! You only look about eighteen.'

'Ten years out.' But it was Amy's turn to stand on the stool and have her hem pinned and tacked. She twirled and turned as directed, and began to feel excited about choosing her blouse to go with the skirt. It was while she was still on her pedestal that Dandy Hall came to visit, with details of the new residents she wanted to bring to Greyrigg.

'Now I know you don't like the idea of Irma's parrot,' she began, her plump goodnatured face flushed with the cold, 'so I've brought Irma and Molly to meet your baby and your dog, so that we can make sure they are all compatible.'

'Molly? Shouldn't it be Polly?' Amy got down from the stool, holding the red velvet gingerly so as not to trip up. 'All right, Dandy, we'll show them round. First meet Sharla, our blushing bride.' And Dandy chatted with the guests and met Mira and the baby.

'Three more is going to keep us busy,' said Hannah. 'Thank goodness two of them are men. Only one more for me in the mornings.'

It was little Aunt Mira who said bashfully, 'Excuse me, Hannah, but I have nothing to do when Shakira is asleep. I am also a trained nurse. If you will allow me, I would like to help.'

This news was greeted with delight. Even Amy had not known that. It meant that the three rooms could be occupied almost at once, and the work load would not be much more. As they all sat over a cup of tea, Ruth said, 'Well, it looks as if everything is going well. The colder the weather, the warmer the hearts inside Greyrigg.'

'Well said! But let's hope as hearts get warmer, the weather doesn't get any worse. I've got to get back to Kilderton.' Dandy collected Irma, who had started chatting to Sarah-Jane, and was paying due respect to her advanced age—which Sarah-Jane loved. 'So you don't mind Molly as well?'

Amy nodded. 'She seems docile enough. We'll give it a try.' And the gay blue and red bird was plainly a diversion that pleased the guests, so perhaps there was no harm in it. 'But we have to be sure the child doesn't get close. Either the perch must be high, or she must be chained to it. Amusing she may be, but don't birds carry diseases?'

'We'll ask Larry,' Dandy decided.

'Isn't he coming today?' Larry had called every single day since the engagement was announced, but the weather seemed against him today.

The preparations for the wedding and the arrival of the new patients meant that Amy had absolutely no time to brood. At night she would lie in bed, go over in her mind the list of things she had to do, and then think of Chris. And because she was so tired, by the time she came to Chris there was only time to pray for him, before she fell asleep. Yet he was there, in her dreams. And she would wake up sometimes with tears on her eyelashes, for things that could never be.

The dresses arrived, and were hung up swathed in tissue and polythene. Amy had taken Edna and Aggie separately to town to choose their blouses. Her own was silk, with ruffles of lace at the sleeves, and Victorian tucks at the front, with a high neck and a silver filigree brooch, provided by the bridegroom. There had been much fuss about gloves—would they or wouldn't they wear them? And hats—Edna thought they were too old to wear flowers in their hair, but changed her mind when she saw the single red rose on a clip, that looked simple and lovely on her grey hair, done gracefully in a chignon instead of its usual plain bun.

The day before the wedding arrived, and Gwyn was the busiest. She had made the cake, of course, but she decided that it was impossible to have too many canapés and savouries. She had made dozens of trays of them, and stocked them in the freezer. Amy had engaged two extra girls to help with the washing up. Amy went upstairs last of all. She paused at Sharla's door. 'Come in, Amy,' Sharla called. She was sitting on the bed. Shakira was fast asleep. The wedding dress hung without its tissue and wrappings, a slim sheath of heavy silk covered with a gossamer layer dotted with silver beads.

They sat and looked at it together. 'Are you nervous, Sharla?' asked Amy.

'No. I'm just so sure that I'm doing the right thing.' Her eyes were shining, 'I just never thought I'd meet anyone so wonderful. I keep hoping I won't wake up and find I was dreaming it.' She turned to Amy. 'Stop me if I'm a bore. I can't see Larry and me ever quarrelling —we are such good friends, as well as——'

'It's just as tremendous for all of us, you know.' Amy wondered why she had always quarrelled with Chris. Obviously because they were never meant to get together. 'It's probably hopeless to say it, but do try to get a proper sleep. And no getting up early! Ruth will bring breakfast in bed, and I'll join you when I've fetched the papers. Not that anyone will read the papers tomorrow!'

'Amy—thank you for everything,' said Sharla earnestly.

Amy suddenly felt choked, and her voice was husky as she said, 'Good night, Mrs Ford.'

'If you called me Your Royal Highness, it couldn't

sound nicer! Good night, Amy.' Amy left her in her pink cloud of roses and bliss. Tomorrow was Sharla's. Nothing must spoil her day—not even Chris. Amy promised herself that she would be so nice that Chris wouldn't even recognise her. But as she fell asleep, she couldn't stop her heart working overtime, in the excitement of knowing she would be seeing him again.

The day started as usual. Amy was grateful for the sun, as she and Nell tramped along in the crisp morning air for the papers, for a chat with Mr Gately, who was as excited as anyone that day, and for a cheery wave from Billy Braithwaite. The roads were as clear as possible for the wedding cars, she noticed. And she was touched to see that some of the villagers had put out their fairy lights early, in honour of the bride. The evergreens were decorated in the gardens too. It was a gesture that delighted Amy, and brought tears to her eyes. 'Oh dear, Nell, I hope I'm not going to cry. I'm starting already!' She shifted the papers to her other hand, and dabbed at her eyes.

She helped Sharla and Mira to dress, before putting on her own outfit, then going in search of her fellow bridesmaids. It was then that she met Chris in the hall, magnificent in morning suit, looking like a film star, as he stood, holding his grey top hat and gloves. They faced each other in a hall strangely deserted. 'Good morning, Chris,' said Amy. 'I thought you might have come last night.'

Impersonal words, to hide her storm of emotion at seeing him. He took a step forward, putting his hat on the sideboard, and took her hands in his. 'I did. I thought you'd be crowded here, so I stayed somewhere else.'

They looked at each other, searching for words. 'You look nice,' he said.

She gave a slight smile. 'So do you.'

The sun slanted its rays in the polished hall, and Amy felt calmer suddenly. She knew Chris had another life. But just for today he was hers, and she was going to enjoy it. He said, 'I've brought a little gift for you. Can I give it you now?'

'Yes. But I must go to Sharla soon.'

He let her hands go and reached inside his pocket, handing her an envelope. 'It's Sarah-Jane's birth certificate—a copy. She wasn't pretending, Amy. She *is* going to be a hundred.'

Amy's reserved manner vanished. 'Oh, Chris, you really are the most wonderful man! How did you manage to think of little Sarah-Jane, in the middle of all your other work! It's the best present I've ever had. Thank you, thank you so much!' And she put her arms round his neck and hugged him.

'And that's the best present I've ever had,' he replied into her ear, and he kissed her cheek several times before she drew away. They looked again into each other's eyes, and it was direct and not formal any more. Chris said, 'See you soon,' and Amy ran upstairs, turning to wave to him, her heart light and happy.

The bridesmaids were driven to the church by Arthur, resplendent as chauffeur of the day. He jumped down and assisted them from the car, being specially gentle with Edna Bell, who had to concentrate, but who walked without a stick, holding Aggie's arm. Her face shone. 'I never thought such a day would come,' she said happily.

'Now don't you cry as well! I'm feeling weepy already.' Amy took her place beside them in the church porch. The red carpet had been put down, for the bride to walk into the church. The organist was playing Bach to his heart's content, the old pipes aged but adequate. Canon Forrester stood at the back of the church waiting for the bride. And Larry in his hired grey sat in the front pew with Chris, handsome under his yellow hair, looking back with a smile and no trace of nervousness for his Sharla to arrive.

The organ broke into a trumpet fanfare, and Larry and Chris stood up before the altar ablaze with chrysanthemums. Then Major Hendon appeared, with Sharla on his arm, head erect, and escorted her with military precision down the aisle in time to the music. Amy walked behind, then Agnes and Edna. The small procession stopped, and the Canon stepped forward. 'Dearly beloved . . .' he began.

Amy listened in a daze, most of her enjoying every word, part of her worrying about Edna standing still for so long. But when she looked, the churchwarden had provided two chairs for the old ladies to sit during the service. And once he had handed Sharla to her husband, the major sat down too. Amy relaxed.

Then the couple went into the vestry to sign the register. Amy gave Sharla back her bouquet, and found herself alongside the best man. They exchanged a smile, and she felt a thrill inside. Surely afterwards they would at last have the chance to speak together, to show they didn't have to be always arguing . . . 'Would you witness the signatures, please?' The Canon was smiling, at having to bring them back to the business in hand. They watched their friends sign their names, then added their own as witnesses. And after kisses and handshakes, they all returned to the crowded little church.

The Wedding March sounded. Sharla put her hand through Larry's arm, and they began to walk down the aisle and out into the sunlight. Amy felt tears threatening again, at the serene happiness on her friend's face. Then Chris was there, bending solicitously. 'Hang on, Amy. You're with me.' And he squeezed her hand protectively as they followed the couple to the door, and were met by flashing cameras and cheers.

Chris helped the three bridesmaids into the next car, then got in the front. 'Have you enjoyed it, ladies?' he smiled. 'Don't worry, I'll look after you. Don't let the photographer bully you to stand up when you don't feel like it.'

Edna said happily, 'I don't know about standing up, I feel as though I could fly!'

While Aggie just sniffed, and said, 'It were just so beautiful.'

While more photographs were being taken in the driveway, Gwyn and her helpers ran inside to take things out of the oven, and put the final touches to the grand buffet. The tables were beautifully arranged, bringing back some of the former glory of the time when the Manor had belonged to one wealthy family, and they habitually used the best silver, and the best linen napkins.

Chris sat next to the bride, and Amy sat next to Chris at the top table. She ate little, feeling a hidden excitement within her. He had stirred her body and soul, and today she would forget that she was bound to get hurt. Today she would take him to her, and ignore any consequences there might be. Today they would be alone, and she would be close to him as she had always wanted to be.

In his speech, Chris was brief, witty, amusing and sincere. And as he traditionally thanked the bridesmaids, Amy was moved by the roar of applause when he mentioned her. She blushed as he referred to all the work she did. And he even described how she had dug away the snow to get Doris to hospital. 'Amy doesn't ask for thanks. She never has. But I know you'd like to say it just today, wouldn't you?' All the guests raised the roof, and Amy felt tears that at last she couldn't control. And Chris, as always, dealt with it gently, lending her his handkerchief, and telling them when it was time to stop. 'And I brought something from St Catherine's House when I came up yesterday that I'll let Amy tell you about,' he went on.

Amy stood up and read out Sarah-Jone's birth certificate. There was more applause, then the guests began to mingle, and gradually the older ones were taken to their rooms for a longer nap than usual.

The sun was low now, across the lake. The bride and groom had been seen off in a Rolls-Royce—Larry's father insisting on paying for it, rather than see them drive away in a Land Rover. Sharla kissed Shakira, and hugged her. Larry took her in his arms, too, and the baby smiled and grabbed at his hair, and showed how perfectly they got on together.

There was activity in the dining room, as the tables were cleared. Amy was last at the door, waving until the car was a long way along the lake road. She felt a hidden shiver of excitement, as she turned and went slowly back to the dining room. Chris would be there. They would share a glass of champagne, and talk quietly, like friends, like lovers . . .

He wasn't in the dining room. Oh well, he was somewhere around; his car was still in the drive. Amy went upstairs to change. She took off the pretty blouse and the red skirt, and put on a dark green woollen dress, with long sleeves and a high collar. She left the silver earrings on, and added the silver brooch Larry had given them all. There. She was ready.

She walked downstairs, listening to the chat among the staff left in the dining room. Then she heard something else—the sound of the engine of the BMW. It was a sound she knew well. She could not mistake it for anyone else. Chris was driving away. Down the drive he went, paused at the road, then accelerated away from her, without looking back.

The sound faded. Amy stood still on the bottom stair. It was as though all the world had collapsed around her with the disappearance of that sound. For a few moments she could not move, not knowing which way to turn or what to do. The hall was full of confetti, and roses from the bouquets and buttonholes lay around, just beginning to wilt a little, though the scent filled the hall.

What an idiot she had been, to think that he really had the time for her! Her heart began to explode with disappointment, with self-criticism, that she could have been so vain as to think Chris cared for her. To have built up her hopes like that. He hadn't said anything that sounded like a promise. He had been nice to her. But then he had driven away, without even saying goodbye. That showed quite clearly what he thought of her. That showed how important she was to him. That should be

her final humiliating lesson. She wasn't even worth a
goodbye.

Gwyn and Mary passed her with trays of dishes. 'Lots
of leftovers in the kitchen, Amy,' they told her. 'Come
and help us finish them off.'

'Right.' Leftovers—that was all she was. Slowly she
unpinned the silver brooch, and took out the earrings,
putting them on the sideboard, next to Aggie's bouquet,
and two empty champagne glasses.

She went to the hall cupboard and dragged out her old
duffle coat and a school scarf. She kicked off her shoes
and put on her wellingtons. Then she went out quickly,
before the girls went through the hall again. She didn't
close the door, merely pulled it to behind her. She thrust
her hands deep in her pockets, as she had forgotten her
gloves, and tramped down the drive, her eyes glazed
with unshed tears. Tramp, tramp, tramp, through the
crisp snow, she heard herself go as though from a long
way away. The boathouse stood across the field, cold
and grey, but sparkling with the last rays of the sun.
There must be more frost on the way. Tramp, tramp
tramp, through the kissing gate and through the trees.
The moon was already showing over Kilderbarrow.

Speedwell now lay upside down, inelegant out of the
water. Amy sat on the bench, hunched up against the
cold—against the world. She knew she was alone here.
She could let herself cry now. The dark water lapped
with a melancholy rhythm on the stone sides of the
boathouse. Bits of ice floated in it. One day spring would
come again—but to Amy, there were centuries of mis-
ery to live through first. Images of the happy day flashed
in her mind, pictures of the laughing bride, of the
dashing best man, on his feet, paying her compliments
that were only empty words, compliments he didn't
mean.

Chris had walked out on her, plain and simple. And
this at a time when her whole being was burning with
love for him, for nothing else in the world but him. Amy
didn't even cover her face now, but cried like a child,

loudly and bitterly, her face contorted with grief. She was alone, and likely to remain so. She knew what it was like to be abandoned, discarded as useless. 'Oh, Chris, how can I bear it . . .?' Had she sobbed the words aloud? What did it matter? Bleak, cold, ice-filled, her life stretched before her, as she faced out towards the moonlit lake, surrounded now by Christmas-card trees as the moonlight touched the frost. In the bleak midwinter . . .

She felt arms go round her, but thought it was her longing imagination. Then through her agony of desolation she began to hear words, as she was slowly drawn tighter into a loving, warm circle, that reminded her of Chris, even though it was only her imagination. 'Don't, love—don't, my love. Oh, Amy love, it's all right, it's going to be all right!'

She slowly turned, her face blotched, red and swollen with crying. He was holding her with one arm, still wearing his morning coat. With the other hand, he was gently wiping the tears from her streaked face. At the sight of him, more tears gushed out, but less raggedly now, more quietly. And as her eyes began to focus a little, she saw that there were tears on his face too, as he murmured to her until she quietened, sniffed and sat silent in the circle of his arm.

Very softly he said, 'You thought I'd gone home?'

She nodded. She had never been a very good liar —and there was no point now; Chris had seen the open depth of her grief and her love. 'I saw—the car——'

'I was in a hurry to get some things for Four Winds before the shops closed. I came straight back, love. I don't think—I honestly didn't expect you to run away. We found your jewellery, and I got very scared. But I had an idea where you'd be and I followed your footsteps.'

She said quietly, 'I just wanted to die.'

'Do you love me as much as that?' His grip tightened.

'You know I do.'

'Fran told me you did. She was furious when I told her the same as you did.'

'You don't have to be nice to me, Chris,' Amy whispered. 'Go on back to your world.'

'Will you come with me?'

She looked at him again. There was no need to care about her face, her hair. But there was a tremulous sincerity in her look as she met his eyes. 'Do you mean it?'

'I do. Will you come?'

'This minute, if you really want me!'

He caught her and held her very tightly. 'I want you so much, darling. I've always wanted you, but you gave me the impression that the Manor came first with you. Why were you always so prickly towards me?'

'I wasn't any good at saying the right thing. And anyway, there was Francesca. She was better for you.'

Chris caught her face in both his hands and kissed her lightly on the lips. 'So you think she's my type? That's an insult to me!'

'I knew I could be your type if you'd let me. I suppose I just didn't dare to think it could work.' Amy clung to him suddenly. 'Oh, Chris, I never knew love hurt so much!'

'Neither did I,' he said fervently.

'I once thought I'd never leave Greyrigg. But I'd go anywhere you asked me. There's nothing left of me any more, you know. Nothing that wants to exist without you.'

He turned her face up to his and wiped a stray tear with his handkerchief. 'Amy, I swear you won't ever cry again. I'll be with you, and I'll never let anything hurt you again, as long as I live.'

'That's a big promise,' she smiled.

'Is it a deal?'

She nodded, just beginning to believe it all. 'I think my life is going to be a permanent Christmas Day,' she told him.

'Talking of Christmas—Four Winds will be finished by then. I thought we'd have a joint Christmas and engagement party, once the decorators have finished.'

'Four Winds?' Amy queried.

'Sorry for not explaining properly. I've sold Harley Street—that's why I had cash for the physio equipment. I've taken rooms in Carlisle, in the same block as Paul Kay. I start in January, when we come back from Quintin's villa in the Greek Islands.'

'We?' echoed Amy.

'You and I. From our honeymoon. You are going to marry me, aren't you?'

'But—you are saying that I won't have to leave Greyrigg?'

'Only in the evenings, my love, when you come home to me.'

Tears filled her eyes. 'Home to you. Oh, Chris——' This time their embrace lasted a very long time. 'You've just described paradise.'

Slowly, small flakes of snow began to fall around them. For a long time they didn't notice. Then Chris drew away, and smoothed the knotted hair back from her eyes. 'Come on, my love. It's been a long day.'

'Where to?'

'Four Winds. You can come back tomorrow for your things. I've got a spare toothbrush.' They smiled at each other, as Amy stood up and brushed down her crumpled coat. He held out his arms, and they walked up the woods together. 'Well, what are you thinking?'

'When I wake up tomorrow, the BMW will still be there, won't it?'

'Naturally. I'll be with you.'

'All night?'

'All my life.'

They stopped at the kissing gate. 'Well, Amy Mac-Farlane, you know what sort of gate this is?' said Chris.

Amy flung her arms round his neck and hugged him to her. They stood for quite a long time in the snow, the flakes melting on the two heads, so close together, lit by a clear white moon.

Doctor Nurse Romances

Romance in modern medical life

Read more about the lives and loves of doctors and nurses in the fascinatingly different backgrounds of contemporary medicine. These are the three Doctor Nurse romances to look out for next month.

ANGEL IN DISGUISE
Anna Ramsay

THEATRE OF LOVE
Lydia Balmain

DOCTOR NEVER DOES
Hazel Fisher

Buy them from your usual paperback stockist, or write to: Mills & Boon Reader Service, P.O. Box 236, Thornton Rd, Croydon, Surrey CR9 3RU, England. Readers in Southern Africa — write to: Independent Book Services Pty, Postbag X3010, Randburg, 2125, S. Africa.

Mills & Boon
the rose of romance

Mills & Boon
COMPETITION

How would you like a
year's supply of Mills & Boon Romances
ABSOLUTELY FREE?
Well, you can win them! All you have to do is complete the word
puzzle below and send it into us by 30th September 1987.
The first five correct entries picked out of the bag after that date
will each win a year's supply of Mills & Boon Romances (Ten
books every month – worth over £100!) What could be easier?

```
M R E T T E L T W I N M
B I T T E R O O R E H A
N C L H A Y V N E E R R
O I G L R S E E E S O R
S T U O S E S S I K D I
O O H Q F A E R T A O A
R X M T E C N S Y N A G
E E N R N L U D A C I E
A F F A I R R R M B R P E
L O M E T E O A L O G W
M O E H A W I S H A O E
R L N M D E S I R E S N
```

Win	Marriage	Kisses	Woman	Mills and Boon
Harlequin	Letter	Fool	Eros	Desires
Romance	Love	Envy	Woe	Realm
Tears	Rose	Rage	Hug	**PLEASE TURN**
Bitter	Wish	Exotic	Men	**OVER FOR**
Daydream	Hope	Girls	Hero	**DETAILS**
Affair	Trust	Vow	Heart	**ON HOW**
				TO ENTER

How to enter

All the words listed overleaf, below the word puzzle, are hidden in the grid. You can find them by reading the letters forwards, backwards, up or down, or diagonally. When you find a word, circle it, or put a line through it. After you have found all the words, the left-over letters will spell a secret message that you can read from left to right, from the top of the puzzle through to the bottom.

Don't forget to fill in your name and address in the space provided and pop this page in an envelope (you don't need a stamp) and post it today. Hurry – competition ends <u>30th September 1987.</u>

Only one entry per household please.

Mills & Boon Competition, FREEPOST, P.O. Box 236, Croydon, Surrey CR9 9EL.

Secret message _____

Name_____

Address_____

_____

_____

_____ Postcode _____